Raba'i al-Madhoun was born in al-Majdal, Askalan, in Palestine in 1945 and grew up in Khan Younis in the Gaza Strip. He moved to London in the 1980s and worked for some of the most prominent Arab-language newspapers. He is currently an editor at the leading Arabic daily, *Al-Sharq Al-Awsat*. The author of several literary works, *The Lady from Tel Aviv* was shortlisted for the Independent Prize for Arabic Fiction in 2010 and is his first work to be translated into English.

Elliott Colla is a prominent translator of modern Arabic fiction, including novels by Ibrahim al-Koni, Ibrahim Aslan and Idris Ali. He currently teaches Arabic literature at Georgetown University, Washington, DC.

Raba'i al-Madhoun

The Lady from Tel Aviv

Translated from Arabic by Elliott Colla

TELEGRAM

Published 2013 by Telegram

I

First published 2009 in Arabic as *al-Sayyida min Tal Abib*
by Arab Institute for Research and Publishing

Copyright © Raba'i al-Madhoun 2013
Translation © Elliott Colla 2013

ISBN 978 1 84659 091 7
EISBN 978 1 84659 122 8

Printed and bound by CPI Group (UK) Ltd, Croydon, CR0 4YY

TELEGRAM
26 Westbourne Grove, London W2 5RH
www.telegrambooks.com

This book has been selected to receive financial assistance from English PEN's Writers in Translation programme supported by Bloomberg. English PEN exists to promote literature and its understanding, uphold writers' freedoms around the world, campaign against the persecution and imprisonment of writers for stating their views, and promote the friendly co-operation of writers and free exchange of ideas.
www.englishpen.org

This novel is dedicated to my wife Sana. And to its characters, Walid Dahman and his mother Amina, Adel El-Bashity and Nasreddine, who lived with us for a full three years.

Prologue

Tomorrow morning Walid Dahman arrives in Gaza. His mother cannot believe the news. She thinks it is just a rumour or legend. Or a fable, like the story of Palestinians returning to their homeland one day.

Each morning she asks herself, 'Will my son come back home before I die? Will I have the chance to tell him all those things I was keeping from him? What will he tell me?'

She has asked herself those questions over and over for thirty-eight years. She listens as the wind whispers the words back to her. She murmurs her disappointments to herself while folding them in the wrinkles and creases of her bedclothes. These are the misgivings she goes to sleep with in the evening. These are the questions she wakes to in the morning. When Walid called from London, she could barely hear him say, 'Mama, I'm coming to Khan Yunis. I'm coming home.' She could not believe it. She did not believe it. Her words ramble on feverishly, and then suddenly, trembling, she blurts out, 'Son—what in heaven's name could be bringing you back here after all these years?'

Walid gets in about 9 am. His visit is no longer just

an idea or possibility. No—he bought his ticket to Tel Aviv. He even chose a flight with an arrival time that would get him there in time to eat breakfast with his mother. *For thirty-eight years she has been making breakfast and setting it out for me every morning. And now the time has finally come to eat it with her.*

He lugs a large suitcase in his right hand, a bag hangs from his left shoulder. He puts his British passport in the shirt pocket right over his heart. He closes the door behind him and begins his journey.

Walid is meeting his mother in an apartment he has never set foot in before. They call it 'the last bachelor pad'. It is a two-bedroom place on the fourth floor. They have made up the room on the street-side for his stay. They put a wooden bed and a wide couch in his room, along with a simple desk where Walid will sit for hours. In the morning, he will surf news sites, skim his email and reply to some of the messages in his inbox. He will also resume work on *Homeland of Shadows*. So many of the details of the book—his fourth novel—hang on how this trip goes.

Something that Walid does not know: in the morning he will rise to the light of a hand-me-down sun that has passed through the Jewish settlement of Nisanit. Gradually he will come to understand this strange phenomenon for what it is, and will do what everyone else does with it. In his dreams, he will wash out the sun. He will do his best to wash away all the shadows of possibility so that the sun stays clean all day long. Yes, as the sun begins to venture off once more into the night, the settlers from Dugit will steal it again. They will grab the sun just before it melts, out there, into the folds of the horizon. When that happens, Walid, like everyone else, will feel the light as it breaks out there, beyond the distant line of barbed wire, outposts and observation towers. When the sun returns again the next morning, it will be wearing clothes cast off by others.

Among the other things that Walid does not know: the last bachelor pad on the fourth floor of the apartment building sits just below the roof, which houses a small poultry farm. His maternal cousin, Nasreddine Dahman, constructed the apartment building during the economic boom of the seventies. In those days, Israel purchased Gazan lives by the year and in bulk. It bought bronzed Gazan forearms licked by the noonday sun and stroked by the salty Mediterranean breeze. In this way, a river of pure Gazan sweat flowed into Israel, irrigating the agricultural sector, mixing into the cement of settlements, and washing the dirty streets clean. That river of sweat was even blended into exquisite cocktails and, some said, used to distil drinking water.

In his day Nasreddine was a hulk of a man. He was tall, with broad shoulders and arms that could lift anything. His hands were so rough he could rub the face off a coin with his bare fingers. When he smashed almond shells against the wall, the explosion could be heard by all eighty thousand inhabitants of the Beit Lahia and Jabalia camps.

Nasreddine used to carry his grandfather's goat on his shoulders. Abbas, his grandfather, had bought the animal so he could rent him out during the mating season. Tan, with honey-brown eyes, that goat had a silky red beard very much like the old man's. Across Nasreddine's massive shoulders, it looked like a kitten.

Nasreddine had a handsome face and the kind of dark skin that women go crazy for. Not that Nasreddine appreciated what he had, or even realized its significance. He hated the colour of his skin and said that it was the dull hue of aubergines. Because of this, he could not stand dishes that contained that swarthy vegetable. And he despised pop songs about tawny beauties—in his mind, they were appalling jingles that only drew more attention to the bad luck of men and women born with brown skin. For roughly the same reason, he loathed Gregor Mendel. Every now and then he would rail at the geneticist, calling him an imbecile who lied and fabricated his evidence. One morning, back in high school, Nasreddine had told his biology teacher that if Mendel's genetic theories were correct, he would have inherited his complexion from his mother and father in equal parts. If the famous Austrian's theories were at all correct, he would have had at least something from his father—like eyes so blue the sea would envy him, or hair fairer than sandy beaches, or the coppery skin of a pomegranate. Nasreddine's teacher laughed and his dark-skinned classmates applauded him.

Nasreddine found employment in many trades.

When the walls of apartment buildings began to go up in the Jewish settlements, it was on his back and shoulders. When Sderot and Rehoboth and Ramat Gan and Ashkelon—not to mention many other Israeli settlements, towns and cities—threw out their rubbish, Nasreddine devoted himself to hauling the stuff away. His hands planted their apple orchards and vineyards, his back heaved crates of export citrus.

Nasreddine would disappear into Israel for a day or more—sometimes for an entire week—selling his day to Israeli taskmasters. When night descended, he would spread out his exhaustion like a mattress and pull the sheets of darkness over him as covers. Over ten years of work, he had managed to save up a few thousand dollars and this enabled him to build a single-storey house for his parents. Over the years, the sweat of his oldest sons raised that house even higher, floor by floor, to the sky. Like him, they had not been able to sell their labour on the local market, and so went elsewhere. In time, the house became a four-storey edifice that took its name from the man who had first built it. Eventually, the Nasrite Building became the envy of many others still standing and others that died, nameless, under the blades of occupation bulldozers.

Walid knows that Nasreddine has seven children. He remembers the names of the five sons, though their identities are scattered in faces he has only ever imagined. And there are two girls who are more like constellations of letters than actual people. This hazy

11

familiarity was a blessing—it allowed him to imagine his cousin's children however he liked, changing their faces and personalities at will. Sometimes he imagined them dark-skinned and sometimes fair, but most often as complete amalgamations. Featureless, they drifted in and out of his imagination. When he grew tired of imagining them this way, he made them out to be perfect replicas of the young Nasreddine and assigned them names at random.

But Walid does know some things for a fact. He knows that Abdelfettah is Nasreddine's eldest—and it is on his account that people call his cousin Abul-Abd. He knows that since birth, Abdelfettah has maintained his position at the head of the siblings list. As the first-born son, he enjoys special status with his father and, with others, a certain respect. Walid also knows that Falah occupied the junior-most rank of Nasreddine's children. They used to call him 'the last grape in the bunch' until he was killed during an incident with an Israeli infantry unit. That happened three years ago on the outskirts of Beit Lahia. When Falah fell off the list, the bunch lost its last. That day the list of Nasreddine's children was revised and Shafiq was reassigned the position of the youngest.

Of Nasreddine's sons, only Shafiq was still a bachelor—and it is in the salon of his apartment that Walid's mother spends most of her time, wallowing in her dread and apprehension. Like a statue of Buddha, she sits cross-legged on a small cotton mattress spread out on a cane mat. Her chin rests directly on her fist. It does not matter whether it is her left fist or her right, since in any case she shifts back and forth from one to the other. Her small head rests right on top, like a small watermelon perched on a bony stick, her elbow buried deep in a thick thigh. She remains like this for a long time and then, when her arms get stiff and tired, she rests them in her lap again.

In this way, Umm Walid goes on hunching over herself. Her contorted poses confirm that certain details of her frame have vanished. Six years ago, when rheumatism began to occupy and settle across her lower limbs, her legs engaged in a unilateral withdrawal. Eventually, they became little more than a horizontal projection from her lower half. Her body began to shrink into itself, as the flesh and fat slowly melted into a shapeless mound around her shanks, until finally all traces of frame and figure had been erased.

Yet Umm Walid's body maintained a chest as wide as a threshing floor and a memory that laughed at forgetfulness. She remembers what Walid told her on the phone that morning, 'Mama, I'm coming to Gaza to visit you.' The words turned her world upside down.

She remembers sharing her doubts with him, 'Are you toying with me, Walid? My boy, are you really going to come back after all these years?' She recalls what she remembers, and still cannot believe it. It is too astonishing to believe, so she tries to call up the scene again.

'Mama, really! I'm coming to Gaza to see you.'

'Anything's possible, son,' she says—and surrenders to the wait.

When her nephews brought Umm Walid to their building about four months ago, she spent the first night at their father's house, as custom would dictate. Ever since, Nasreddine's sons have vied with one another to play host to their father's aunt. They love her dearly as an aunt inherited from their father and as an adopted grandmother for their young ones. The young children's maternal grandmothers had all disappeared some time ago, swallowed up somewhere amidst the closures, curfews, checkpoints, aerial bombardments and recurrent ground offensives—not to mention the chaos of the Palestinian Authority and the militias.

Zuhdiyya, Nasreddine's mother and their paternal grandmother, had a stroke that left her half paralysed the day her grandson Falah was killed. Now she spends what remains of her days in a bed in a corner of her son's apartment. This woman, who used to do all the laundry for the nine people in the family by hand, now waits, with some shame and embarrassment, for the person who will someday come to wash and say prayers over her dead body. The young children only have one real grandmother now, Ruqiyya, Nasreddine's wife. There are fourteen of them, girls and boys; the oldest is not even six, and the youngest has yet to let out his first real scream. Since there are so many of them, the kids have little chance of getting even a hug from her.

When Umm Walid arrived it was with a warm breast broad enough to hold them all in a single loving embrace. But she changed when her legs stopped working and has now become a kind of radio whose volume and frequency are difficult to modulate. Compensating in talk and chitchat for what she has lost in terms of bipedal ambulation, nowadays she gets around mainly by way of tongue and lips and words. One day, two months after she arrived at the Nasrite Building, deluging them with informative programmes, Emad, Nasreddine's second son, put forward the following proposal to the younger Nasrites, their wives, sons and daughters: they would implant an electronic chip in a small incision just under her tongue. The chip would help them adjust the broadcast function by remote. They could thus control the volume on their aunt in a convenient, fully civilized manner, or even turn off the torrent of words if necessary. For instance, you might want to change the channel so as to listen to Israeli bullets, aimed precisely to hit any Gazan that had the misfortune of standing in their way. (Then again, perhaps those pedestrians are the lucky ones, since at least in death they might find mercy and rest?) Or you might instead prefer to listen to the ricochets of bullets fired by true patriotic Palestinian militias, competing against one another to provide security, peace and calm? Or maybe you want to listen to something else, like the ululations of women cheering newlyweds to victory and triumph on their wedding night, as in the great conquests of times past?

But everyone began to worry about what might happen to their aunt if she were to undergo this risky surgical operation. Emad reassured them, in the smooth confident voice of a doctor in a white lab coat, 'Medicine has come a very long way, everyone. God willing, we can also have it inserted, free of charge, in Shafa Hospital here in Gaza. For your information, I will be there personally to supervise the procedure.'

The proposal was received with a roar of laughter, and they applauded their aunt, who would become the first woman in the Gaza Strip to be operated by remote control.

Despite the relief Umm Walid felt at their welcome, she was still prisoner to feelings of exile and uprootedness. *The further from home you go, the smaller you appear,* she murmured to herself. When she whispered to herself, she did so in instalments because if you speak to yourself continuously and without interruption, you cannot take real pleasure in the words themselves. She knew her homelessness was of an honourable kind. For one thing, her exile was not extreme—it was like that of the people of Acre who were expelled not out of the city entirely, but only to its outskirts. In any case, age-old protocols stipulated that when marrying, a bride must move from her family's home to the groom's. Despite all this, she could be counted on to bring up 'the story of her house' at any point, as if it might dispel these awful feelings.

Umm Walid's house was, and still is, the last thing she possesses in a world whose time is about to fold up on her. She has no husband around, nor children. The only thing that has stood by her has been this home of hers. She loves it dearly and is quite possessive about it. Whenever she is alone with her home, she talks to it, reaching her fingers to the nearest wall as if to caress the features of a beloved friend. Sometimes she stretches and leans back in the tiny sitting room. That is the only position that allows her body to stretch out fully and her eyes to wander far and wide like two skiffs lost at sea. She stares up at the slanted, rickety ceiling made of thick sheets of asbestos, and she whispers a little prayer for her house. 'May God protect you and make you strong, just as you have protected me.' She rolls onto her side—either side, it does not matter which—and puts her ear to the ground. She listens carefully to how the house breathes. Its breath comes and goes like the soft whisper of a breeze carrying stories from beyond the hills—or is that sound the pulsing of her heart?

She used to speak to her house all the time, complaining to it, listening to its complaints. Each night, she would dream of laying tiles across its old floor. She dreamed of painting its doors sea-blue, and its walls such a bright chalky white that on moonless nights the house would light up the entire alley. One day, she watched as her dream awoke and came true. The Nasrite boys made their aunt's vision a reality—tiling the floor, painting the walls and its little wooden door exactly as it had been in her dream. Her house became a wedding gown. That is, until an Israeli missile threw a mourning shawl over it. The roof was thrown to the wind. Parts of the walls collapsed. Most of the sparse possessions inside went up in flames.

Umm Walid abandoned her house for internal migration—it was the fourth such time she had done so in her life. During this time she went back to collecting all the old stories, making them into a single master narrative: 'Our first house, where Walid was brought up, was razed by Sharon's tanks in 1970. The Jews did that to widen the streets. They did that so they could use jeeps and armoured cars to hunt down the resistance. An Israeli shell fell on our second house during the Sharon era. I cleaned up all the rubble, shrapnel and splinters—then I rebuilt the place and plastered it. Not six months went by when an Apache helicopter fired a rocket into it. It landed right in my flour sacks. Every piece of furniture was destroyed, and a white cloud of flour filled the sky. As God is my witness, the place stood there empty, without a roof or furniture, until my brother's sons rebuilt it for me. Abdelfettah, Emad and Shafiq put in the floor, they painted it and fixed it up. I went back to live in the house. Four months later I was sitting on the front doorstep when all of a sudden that Apache comes back. It's hovering over us and making a racket. I say, "Lord, protect us!" Where do you think he's going to shoot this time? No one's around, except for a couple of Hamas twerps. One of them's got a rifle, the other's carrying something like a water pipe. They're trying to hide themselves right in front of me in the alley—so I start yelling at them, "What do you think you're doing, boys? Don't you have any better place to go? People live here, you know—and now they're going to shoot at us!" As soon as I say this, the missile hits. I watched myself do two somersaults through the air and land far from the house. It was God's mercy that the missile landed inside the house, or I would have died along with those two boys. This was the fourth time that my house was destroyed by Sharon. God damn Sharon and everything to do with him—does he think my house is a military post, a training camp? Every time I build a new house, he blows it up—does he think that Hamas leaders follow me around each time I move?'

In the last bachelor pad, Umm Walid spends the night with no one to keep her company. She tosses and turns in bed for hours, and the hours toss and turn with her. Just before midnight, Emad, the last of them to go to sleep, hears her voice as he walks by the apartment door—and it makes him freeze where he is standing. 'Abu Nasreen, may God keep you safe tomorrow morning when you go to pick up Walid at the Erez crossing. Please let them leave us in peace. Just for a little bit. My heart's been full of worry ever since he went away. I want my heart to be as clean and bright tomorrow as the laundry I washed for him the day he left.'

Emad closes the apartment door behind him. In silent obedience to Umm Walid's wishes, he takes his leave.

She shuts eyes heavy with images of the past. Shadows from that last day come rushing back to the surface.

Departure

His mother had finished washing the clothes he would take with him back to Cairo. She was getting ready to hang them on the clothesline when her question halted him in his tracks: 'Walid, where you going this morning?'

His whole body tensed and a sudden sense of dread made him stop at the front door. *God—what does she want from me this morning?* The subtext of her question would always come out, eventually.

'If you're going out, boy, why don't you take a couple of rabbits with you to sell at the market?'

He hated rabbits. He hated buying rabbits and he hated selling them. He hated slaughtering them and he hated eating their meat, even when it was served, Egyptian-style, in mulukhiyya soup. Most of all, he hated this question: 'Walid, where you going this morning?' He thought of that day, not so long ago, when his mother had sprung that same question, only it was a different time of day. 'Walid, where you going this evening?' He stood there then, as he stood there now, waiting. That night she had not hesitated for a moment to ask him to come with her to visit the family of another relative, Amin Dahman, who had just passed away. She wanted them to offer their condolences to his many children and grandchildren, even though they needed no consoling. That night, Walid listened to what was said—what had already been said hundreds of times at other services. 'He was—may God have mercy on him—a such and such kind of man. He did all this, and he did all that …' However, Amin Dahman was not a person about whom anything good could be said. The man was a total cheapskate—stingy and spiteful until his dying breath. He was a pathological liar. He lied more often than the average Arab leader, especially the kind who claimed he would stop at nothing to liberate Palestine. He was the kind of man to whom no one should show mercy when he died. The kind of man about whom you might say, 'God, please send the old fart straight to hell!'

Despite all this, men thronged to offer their condolences when Amin Dahman died. On the way to the service, they began revising the scripts they were reading from and whispering among themselves that the dearly departed deserved the compassionate thoughts of one and all. They prayed that he would be granted forgiveness and mercy in the hereafter.

Umm Walid offered her condolences to the departed's womenfolk: a handful of sobs pouring into a lake of tears shed by other women. These were women who wept in genuine grief when others suffered loss.

That day, Walid vowed to himself never to attend the funeral of his own father when he died. It would be enough for him to offer and receive his own private condolences. He did not want to have to hear hollow platitudes about his father. When his father did die, he remembered none of these promises. For three straight days, Walid sat submissively listening to every nice word that was said about his father.

Walid turned to face his mother. 'Mama—I'm not going anywhere.'

A smile appeared on Umm Walid's face. She knew that he would not leave the house before listening to what she had to say.

She bent over the laundry tub, taking a big cotton towel in her hands and wringing it out. A scented cloud of lye detergent wafted up through the house. From a cotton bag, she took out two wooden clothes pegs, putting one in her mouth while throwing the towel onto the clothesline. She put the other peg on one edge of the towel. With her tongue stuck behind her teeth, she said, 'Yefteyay, uh fawhhh youyy faffer imm a drumm.'

He laughed at the sound of her tongue tripping over the clothes peg. She snatched it out of her mouth and clipped it onto the other edge of the towel. 'Yesterday, I saw your father in a dream. God bless the man. You know, he was asking about you.'

Thank God my father hasn't forgotten me, Walid whispered to himself.

'He asked about you three times.'

Walid tried to shift the subject away from the dream. 'Did you tell him it's my last year in college and that I'm going to graduate?'

But she would not be diverted. 'You should go tell him that yourself. Go visit him and recite the Fatiha over his grave—he'll help you find your reward.'

Recklessly—in a mere two words—he took up the challenge, muttering, 'Won't/Dontwanna.' He turned to go, then paused when he thought of the dusty old dictionary where she kept her curses. He could already imagine her saying, 'He won't/dontwanna? I'll dontwanna, boy!' He does not know which won't/dontwanna she would use on him—but he knows that when she starts to won't/dontwanna him, he is going to lose all feeling in his body.

The fear he felt toward his mother's won't/dontwanna made him revise his words. 'Mama, the morning's still young. I'll make sure to go to his grave later.'

'Does the memory of your father mean so little to you?'

'Mama, Father's dead, God have mercy on him. I have to go right now. I have to go to the market to buy some things for my trip.'

'If you don't go visit your father's grave now, the whole day will come and go—and you'll have lost your chance.'

She bent over the laundry tub again. She took out a dress shirt and, in her agitation, threw it roughly on the line. 'Go see him right now. Go.'

'OK. I'm going.' He muttered to himself, *As long as my father's asking after me, I will go and ask after him.*

Walid closed the door behind him. He walked along, intending to go just about anywhere or do just about anything other than start his day with a morning visit to the city's dead. He had only taken a few steps when his mother's voice caught up with him: 'Listen to your mother, Walid.'

*

Walid thought about going to the market. But his thoughts were sidetracked by the familiar spectre of the barber Said Dahman, with his skinny lamppost frame and unruly curls flying in the wind. Using water infused with lime leaves, Said was washing down the cement bench in front of his barbershop. By the time the barber had finished carefully arranging the cushions on the bench, the air was saturated with the fragrance of spring and the place had taken on the appearance of a tourist spa. Said sat down and lit himself a cigarette, and let the resort appeal of the place do the work of pulling in customers from the main street.

The scene pulled Walid in. He drifted toward the shop where he knew his friend—and cousin—would welcome him warmly. 'May your day be nothing but jasmine! All blessings on you, my magnificent friend!' He would then start to tell Walid a great new story that would, like the fingers of dawn touching a flower, gently pry open his heart. And Said would assure him, as he always did, that he has never told this story to anyone else before. Then he would make Walid promise not to repeat it, since he might need to tell it again sometime, in the event he ran out of stories.

Walid referred to him as 'Bard of the Camp', and Said responded enthusiastically to the grandiose title. He gathered the stories of the camp from the lips of his customers and from others. He washed some of the sentimentality out of them to distil the essence of the words. Then he would add his secret blend of salacious innuendo. When it finally came out as a story told to his customers, it was always presented as brand new. Said would swear a thousand times over that it had never been told before.

Walid remembered that he'd already promised to meet Said in the evening. Their mutual friend Fawzi Ashour would be joining them too, and that was a sure sign they'd hear a newly minted fable. Or, if not exactly new, it would be one that had at least been cleaned and pressed in Said's inimitable fashion. When Walid remembered all this, he changed his mind about going over to see him now. *It's not possible*, he thought to himself, *it's not possible to listen to Said's banter twice in one day, not even if it's juiced up with irony and outrageous exaggerations*. The thought gave him comfort and he turned away.

Suddenly, there was his mother's voice again: 'Listen to your mother, Walid.' It occurred to him that he might try tricking his way out of the visit to his father's grave with some brazen lying: 'Oh yeah, Mama. I went to visit Dad today, and recited the Fatiha over his grave … He seems to be in excellent shape, by the way. He was wearing his old navy blue suit—the one with the grey pinstripes. Oh, and another thing: he gave me my allowance, right from his own pocket. He told me to say a big hello.'

What if she believed it and asked him to tell her more? *'Don't hide anything from your mother, Walid! What advice did your father give you?'*

He would tell her, 'Sparks were shooting out of his eyes and he asked me: "Has your mother remarried since my death, Walid?"' The woman would lose the last bits of sanity she still had.

Yet, in that moment, his mother would not miss a beat. No, she'd reach into a store of curses so rare she only pulled them out on special occasions like this. 'Want your mother wed? You'll soon be good and dead. You'll be buried before I'm married, boy. Go bury yourself next to your father and give me a break.'

The image in his mind made him laugh out loud. *My mother is unbelievable—and so is that big bag of words she carries around. If you say, 'Wedlock,' she might reply, 'Gets you in a headlock.' Say, 'I'm going …' and she might reply, 'To hell in a handbasket?' Say, 'We're off …' and she might answer, 'To choke on your own drool?' Say, 'I'm falling asleep, I'm going to bed,' and she might declare, 'Hope the wall falls asleep on top of you!' And do not say, 'Mama, I'm on my way …' because she will definitely quip: 'To your funeral? Let's go together!'*

But when your mother is happy with you, her words turn from lead to gold. Say, 'I'm going …' and she'll reply, 'To be happy and secure in life!' Say, 'I'm going to go …' and she will say, 'To Heaven, my dear?' 'I'm on my way …' becomes 'To your wedding? We'll go together—and I'll sing for you, the happy groom!'

Fine. And when your mother asks you about the others you saw paying their respects at the graveyard? You are going to have to lie once or twice at the very least. And if you don't get the story straight, you'll get whacked by your mother's bag of words!

Walid thought it over gloomily before he finally decided, *Forget it, Walid. A visit to your father will spare you a visit from your mother's tongue.*

He continued walking until he reached the main street. When he got to the seed market, he leaned up against a wall and lit a Rothmans' cigarette. He began to watch the scene in front of him through clouds of smoke.

He was about to leave. But when Mona suddenly appeared, he froze. Mona's real name was Abdelhamid Awed. The city and its camps refused to recognize him as a gay man. Instead, they talked about him as a her. Mona was carrying one of the old black radio batteries on his left shoulder while walking, as people did, to the gas station at the roundabout. That was the only place where you could get batteries recharged.

Walid trembled. A deluge of old shame washed over his body. *Why is Mona here, now? Why is that faggot so determined to damage my reputation? It only happened once, and that was a mistake. What does he want from me now?*

He took a deep drag from the cigarette trembling in his fingers, and then exhaled it like a heavy load of remorse. *Why did you have to mess with him, Walid?* You used to hate the boys who talked dirt, and you used to keep your distance from the kids in the alley. Your father used to call out to you from his room while you were playing in the street. He would yell: 'Don't play with those dirty kids, Walid!' Your father's words were sacred. He did not have to yell more than once for you to listen. What would you say to your father if he came back from the grave and heard what was going around? *Do you want to kill your father all over again, Walid?*

It had happened one stormy autumn evening. Gusts of wind blew the pedestrians and loiterers off the streets and alleys. They swept off all the chickens, cats and dogs too. As soon as Walid was sure that no one would see him, he had hurried along, his hands gripping the edges of his open wool jacket while the wind grabbed and played with it. He'd set off behind Mona at a short distance without ever taking his eyes off him. Walid had watched the man walking with the coquettish saunter of a peasant girl carrying a clay water jar on her head. His hips swayed back and forth as he walked. Meanwhile, Walid trembled, unsure of himself. More than once he thought about going back. In the end, it was not Walid, but desire that finally made the decision, and dragged him beyond risk. When, at last, they got to the culvert down by the fields, Walid could not restrain himself any longer. He gave in, and let himself be drawn to Mona's neck. There, where the empty water pipe was nearly one metre deep beneath the train tracks, four hundred metres down from the Khan Yunis train station, the sound of Walid's heaving breath was lost in the whistling of the winds. The trembling of his body melted in the shadows of the pipes.

Walid's eyes filled with tears as he trembled again, apologizing to his father.

*

Walid threw his cigarette butt down on the ground and continued on his way to the graveyard. Within minutes, he was standing in front of his father's grave, silently declaring his submission to the sovereignty of death. *In the name of God, the Compassionate, the Merciful...*

This mound of cement is the resting place of Ahmad Nimr Dahman.

This is my father. An exact replica of myself, only older. His medium height, his slight build, his complexion, his piercing eyes (which people say that I also have, though I do not believe it). His temper, a tension in the body that you could almost smell. The way he walked, like he was marching in a military parade. I inherited all this from him. Anyone who knew my father would look at me twice and say, 'This must be Ahmad Dahman's son.'

My mother used to say, 'You're the spitting image of your father. Your hair, your eyes, your nose, even that chin of yours, dimpled like a Palestinian penny. The spitting image. When you get mad, your face turns red like his did and you start to rant and rave until none of us can understand a word you're saying. But the way your throat tightens when you get mad—that part comes from me. You know, Walid, if one day you were to leave me and go away and not come back until you'd grown as old as he was—God have mercy on him—you know what? I'd probably say, "This is Ahmad, not Walid."'

God have mercy on the man.

Ahmad Nimr Dahman had been an employee at the UNRWA distribution centre. In his youth, he had been a handsome, educated and gentle man. Wherever he went, people loved him.

On that July day when it was too hot to even talk, some of Ahmad's co-workers had accused him of stealing clothes from the depot and smuggling them out via friends of his on the staff. The matter was brought to the attention of the director, Khamis al-Sawafiri, who promptly ignored it, saying that what had gone missing was not worth the bother of an investigation. But the thefts continued. When containers of food started to disappear every day, new accusations were born.

At the end of a week filled with more thefts and finger pointing, the director decided to put an end to it all. He sent a hand-written letter to Ahmad Dahman, accusing him of the thefts, and notifying him to stay home from work until they had completed an investigation into the matter.

Ahmad fired off a volley of complaints to the head of UNRWA in Gaza City. All of these memos were forwarded to his former boss—and became part of the file. In less than two weeks, Ahmad joined the unemployed, where he was warmly embraced by the prospect of life without sustenance. On the rasp-like tongues of the camp, the 'Respectable Family of Abu Walid' became the 'Detestable Family of All Thieves'.

After losing his job and the respect of all, he did not survive for even a month. It was an eternity for him. Then something happened that took everyone by surprise. One morning, as he went off to Café Mansour in the city centre, he was followed by the spectre of death. Death chased after Ahmad Dahman as if it were hustling through a jam-packed schedule of appointments and interviews. It did not come for the man before he left his house in the morning. Nor did it wait for him to come home. It did not even wait for the poor man to finish drinking the mint tea he had ordered when he got to the café. No, Death arrived right then in the form of a massive heart attack that twisted his arteries before wringing them out again. When it happened, Abu Walid's body shot up rigid, his right hand clutching at his left arm. He screamed in pain as he collapsed back into the bamboo chair. All the customers crowded round him, as did all those drawn to the scene by his shrieks. Ahmad Dahman breathed his last and died while his cup of tea was still piping hot. Carried on mint-laced wafts of steam, the man's soul rose into the air and evaporated for ever.

After his death, Umm Walid became increasingly agitated and forgetful. Sometimes she would lose all consciousness of what was happening around her. She would sit in silence at the door to her bedroom for hours on end. Sometimes she would bring the chickens out from their cages, calling out, 'Ta-ta-ta-ta-taaa,' while she threw handfuls of barley on the ground. The chickens would race to snatch up the grains. She would sit and watch as they wiped their beaks on the ground and turned to beg for more. She would talk to them as if she were talking to neighbourhood women and confiding all her secrets: 'They killed him. Those thieving sons of bitches murdered him. They were the ones stealing bags of food and splitting them up among themselves. Abu Walid must have been standing in their way, threatening to go public. Then they decided to get rid of him. God damn those sons of ...!'

One day, about three months after Ahmad Dahman's death, Walid's grandfather, Nimr, asked Walid to accompany him when he went to the market to buy some tobacco. He told his grandson that the local farmers sold a wide variety at half the price the stuff went for in shops. He also told him he liked to mix different kinds together in ways that the cigarette factories could not manage. He beamed and bragged that his blend was as good as Rothmans and Kent and Craven A—maybe even better. He swore that his blend was better than the local brand Si Salem.

The two walked down the main street. Walid listened intently as his grandfather talked about the scents and flavours of all the various kinds of cigarettes. Since tradition dictated that Walid would never light one in the presence of the patriarch, his pleasure was confined to talking about them.

'Walid, my son, do you know Khamis al-Sawafiri? Khamis is the one who was doing all the stealing. I heard that he had a fight with your father over a woman from Jaffa named Sawsan al-Ghandour. They say she is a beauty. Khamis had his eye on this woman. And some say—though only God knows if it's true—that she had her eye on your father. Khamis started to steal the stuff from the distribution centre and one of his employees pointed the finger at your father. When Khamis fired your father, he planted the sickness in your father's heart that eventually killed him. You know what, son? I never believed for one second that my son had anything to do with this Sawsan or any other lady. I am his father and I knew him better than anyone else.'

That is what Walid's grandfather told him.

The story so stunned Walid he could only stutter, 'If I'd known, I would have killed him.'

'No, son. No, Walid—let God wreak His vengeance on those who oppress others.'

Walid looked at the cement grave. He stared at the shadows dancing on the leaves of the tree above. Here and there above the grave, small bags hung from branches. They fluttered in a breeze infused with the dankness of graveyard soil and the thirsty perfume of the desiccated wildflowers that grew here and there.

A sudden gust flew up and the leaves of a low branch brushed against Walid's forehead. Walid turned to look and was surprised to see a delicate handkerchief hanging in the branches. It was embroidered with a design and in colours used by lovers, and flickered coyly in the wind. Walid forgot his anger at the wind and began to listen to a nervous voice inside. Did his mother tie a handkerchief to a tree branch every time she visited the grave? Or was it Sawsan who had decorated the tree above Ahmad's head?

Wounded with doubt, he looked again at the grave. Did my father do that? Were he and Sawsan al-Ghandour in love? But he always used to say that my mother was the brightest flower of the Dahman girls. My mother, whose soul was torn into pieces the day he died and distributed to all the other mourners. It is horrible to think he might have been in love with someone else. True, my mother's got a temper and a mouth as foul as a sailor's. But she is beautiful and kindhearted. And to this day she still swears oaths on his life, as if he had never died.

Around him, the wind whispered like a faint moan from the beyond. Walid heard a voice repeating, 'Think

35

about your mother, Walid.' Walid knew it was his father's voice.

He recited the Fatiha and rushed out of the graveyard.

*

On his way back, Walid passed by Hafiz al-Batta's shop. He bought some ballpoint pens, shampoo, toothpaste and socks—everything he would need in Cairo but knew he would not easily be able to find. He took all his purchases home and left them there, then went back out to say goodbye to his friends, starting with the three Muhammads, as he liked to call them: Muhammad, whose mother was Khadija, Muhammad al-Misriyya, whose mother was Egyptian, and Muhammad, whose family name was Samoura.

Muhammad Khadija lived right behind Walid's house in a cluster of homes that also housed the families who had fled the village of Beit Daras in 1948. To get there, Walid had only to head west and quickly double back at the corner.

He knocked on the door three times. Muhammad's mother, Khadija, called out to him from inside, 'Come on in, Walid. It's not like you're a stranger.'

Walid pushed the door open and the rusty hinge began to squeal. He walked inside and called out a greeting that was interrupted by one from Umm Muhammad: 'Welcome, welcome! Come in, Walid!'

Umm Muhammad turned and disappeared back

into her kitchen, where she began to make tea for them.

Muhammad was about the same age as Walid. At first, it had been childhood games that brought the two boys together. Like his father, Hassuna Rayyan, Muhammad suffered from weak eyes—and now, like his old man, it was easy for him to remain, in good standing, a full member of the unemployed club. Muhammad had the same handsome wide eyes as his mother, only his were clouded over by the ash-grey hues of his father's. At that time, all that kept Muhammad from being completely blind were the two speck-holes from which he peered onto a world he saw only in miniature.

Muhammad had never been able to enrol in school. Separated from an education by two small clouds of ash, he never learned to read or write. Those clouds hung in the sky over every school he approached. Muhammad's father knocked again and again on the gates of various schools to let the boy in, but they never opened.

Years went by and Muhammad's eyes narrowed and tightened until his sight began to sputter and choke. Finally one day they tasted their last gasp of light and stopped breathing. After that, Muhammad began to see things with his fingers instead. He began to recognize people by the sound of their voice and the noises they made. Walid was not imagining that when he approached—even when he did not make a sound—Muhammad would somehow sense his

37

presence, perhaps by perceiving his scent from far off.

Khadija was teasing her son when Walid walked in. 'When he lost his eyes, he grew the snout of a dog. He knows your scent, Walid.'

Muhammad stretched out both of his hands to shake both of Walid's. They always used to greet each other this way, as if they were four and not two people. Muhammad replied, 'The only scents I can smell from far away, Mama, are the scents of good people.'

Each of them took a sip of their mint tea. Then they gulped down their drinks, as if they were hurrying off to another appointment, took their leave and went out.

The two friends wandered through each alley as if they were surveyors sent to measure every corner of the neighbourhood. Walid began to fill the empty spaces with stories of his experiences in Cairo. He talked to his friend about Cairo's dark-skinned girls with their bare legs and paper-thin skirts. Muhammad would listen entranced, filling in the details with the letters of the words.

Walid told him about his studies, about his failure to be admitted to the archaeology department at Cairo University, and how he'd been forced to enrol in history instead.

Ever since he was a child, Walid had been crazy about antiquities. He was in love with their mystery and the secrets they contained. He would often go to the Imam al-Shafi mosque in Gaza. He would pray as soon as he stepped foot inside, performing an extra prostration each time. Then he would sit like a pious devotee, studying the interior of the mosque, trying to glean the imprints of history from the ornaments on the ceiling and the surfaces of the pillars and walls.

Walid would tell his stories while Muhammad listened, spellbound. To signal his astonishment at what he heard, Muhammad would say nothing more than, 'There is no god but God!' To express his amazement, he would shout, 'God is great!'

Walid told Muhammad stories about the pyramids of Giza and the Sphinx. He told him about his first visit to the Great Pyramid and the Pyramid of Cheops and how, upon entering, he had been forced to bend over as he scrambled along a low passageway lit by electric bulbs. He told him how his feet padded softly across a staircase of wood and rope.

Walid recounted the incident in a whisper, the words streaming breathlessly from his lips. Muhammad was right there, breathlessly scampering after him. There was Walid, pulling on the rope, just as Muhammad was reaching for it in his imagination, his feet stretching to feel for the stairs beneath them. And the two friends climbed up and up until they reached the end of the tunnel.

In that place, in the presence of the great Pharaoh whose embalmed life had been stolen by ancient thieves, the two friends stood up proudly and swaggered beneath the vaulted ceiling. For hours, they studied the granite sarcophagus. Together, they read the bas-reliefs and, using nothing but their intuition, began to translate the texts they found.

Walid told Muhammad about the hieroglyphs of the Pharaohs and about the many ancient words still employed by modern Egyptians. Muhammad would repeat after him, 'Sah. Dah. Embo. Kaa. Kukh. Bah. Mmiim. Nnuun. Ti. Ti. Ti. Nef. Rah. Rah. Nef. Rah. Ti. Ti. Nefrahtiti. Nefrehtiti. Who's Nefretiti, Walid?'

'She was a queen. Nefertiti was the wife of the Pharaoh Akhenaton. Her name means "the Beauty to Come."'

'You mean, she was good-looking?'

'Something like that.'

Walid began to describe the Beauty to Come to his friend. With letters and words, he painted the most striking aspects of her physiognomy. Muhammad drank all this in and tucked it away in his memory. When Walid had finished telling the story of the beautiful queen, Muhammad leaned his head back and slightly to the left, as if he were searching for her in the shadows of his eyes. Then he broke into a beaming smile and shouted, 'My God—she is so damn beautiful!' His fingers began to draw precise sketches in the air. Before Walid's eyes, the form of the queen began to take shape, the silhouette of a crystalline idea created in the hands of a sightless sculptor. The figure of the queen hung there in the air in front of them, and the details of her marble body began to quicken. As soon as Muhammad had formed her body with the clay of his mind, the beautiful queen began to parade right before their very eyes. As she had done at the bedside of the young king thousands of years before, she danced, offering up her nude ebony skin and fine Nubian features.

Walid stopped in his tracks, his feet suddenly nailed to the ground. 'Muhammad, you're an amazing sculptor. It's exactly like her. I promise, when I come back from Egypt, I'm going to bring you a statuette of Nefertiti. And then you can decide which is more beautiful, the queen I bring you, or the one you just made in your mind!'

The two friends roared with laughter, delighted by their game of carving statues out of thin air.

*

Walid said goodbye to Muhammad Khadija and went over to the neighbourhood across the way. At the corner, he bumped into his friend, Muhammad al-Misriyya, the son of Fathiyya the Egyptian and Adnan al-Badrasawi, the neighbourhood's most infamous chicken thief. Whenever a chicken went missing, its feathers would invariably appear the next morning just outside the front gate to their house. Adnan's wife would have dumped them there, publicizing the fact that they had supped on borrowed fowl the night before.

Muhammad was a shoeshine. At this hour, he usually sat on his flimsy wicker stool, right behind his case of shoe polishes, creams and dyes. He would watch the feet of passersby and study their shoes, muttering under his breath at anyone who wore sandals, even on hot summer days.

Subhi al-Nabrisi was an old classmate of Walid's, and Muhammad so admired the guy's shoes that more than once he just about fell in love with them. He used to say, 'Subhi's shoes are really good-looking. They're cute—like baby booties.' In contrast, he despised a boy called Fathi al-Sinwar, and cursed the day he had come to Muhammad asking for a full-service shine. The shoes that Fathi set down on Muhammad's box were not exactly footwear. They were more like two leaky sabots whose hulls had blown out from stern to aft.

Muhammad left school when he turned nine, before he'd managed to complete third grade. Since that time, he had always worked shining shoes so as to add a few coins to what his father brought in working seasonally in the fields.

Muhammad was also an epileptic. Whenever he had a fit, his mind would drift into unconsciousness while his body was gripped by convulsion. His mouth would spew mounds of frothing drool and foam would collect around his lips. Whenever this occurred, everyone instantly became an expert on epilepsy and would rush over to gawk at Muhammad's thrashing body. Someone would invariably jab a knife into the dirt next to Muhammad's head. The crowd of experts would then listen to the screams of the devils that inhabited Muhammad's body. They would watch the dying demons rushing out of him, scrambling over the froth on his lips. By the time the fit was over, all traces of affliction would vanish and so too all those epilepsy experts, taking their rituals and their talismans with them. When Muhammad came to again, he would be shaken and confused. He could never understand why his lips were covered in a sticky lather, or why his clothes were dirty. He was always surprised to find that someone had tossed his little stool so far away.

Now Walid stood over Muhammad, his right shoe resting on Muhammad's box. Muhammad lifted his eyes and looked closely at Walid for a moment, then said ruefully, 'Going away, my friend? I already know. I want to shine your shoes until they're as bright as mirrors. All you'll need to do is wear your green pinstriped suit, the kind those Egyptian broadcasters wear, and all the girls in Cairo will be chasing after you. Give me your other shoe, Walid. This time it's on the house—in honour of your return to the university.'

Walid let him do it. After finishing his shoes, Muhammad stood up to say goodbye to his friend. Walid hugged Muhammad al-Misriyya tightly and left a silver coin on his box. Then he went off, determined to meet the last of the three Muhammads.

*

At nightfall, Walid met up with Muhammad Samoura just as he was returning from work. Muhammad had been a lazy tailor but was now a cop, chasing thieves through the camp.

Walid knew that Muhammad would not pass up the

43

opportunity to sit around and talk after work. When he got off his shift, Muhammad could be found in front of Jaber Rayyan's little shop letting loose with heroic sagas about how he chased robbers or how he had caught some of the most wanted criminals. During the winter break, unemployed kids would spend their days and nights there, listening and retelling their own stories of unsuccessful romantic adventures.

When Muhammad saw Walid, he left his audience and went to greet his friend. They shook hands and walked away without saying much. Muhammad had already fired off all the narrative ammunition in his clip. And Walid just wanted to get home and pack the clothes his mother had washed that morning, along with the stuff he had bought.

Walid said farewell to Muhammad as the other went on his way toward the upper camp, behind Mustafa Hafez Elementary School. Walid hurried home.

*

Muhammad Samoura was the only one of his old friends that Walid had heard anything about in recent years. People said he was no longer the policeman Walid had known more than forty years ago. He had begun to receive regular promotions and moved up through the ranks. With the white armband and stripes on his right shoulder, Muhammad would strut about the streets, parading all his shiny badges and medals. When the

Palestinian Authority was set up under Yasser Arafat's leadership in May 1994, Muhammad was assigned to the Preventive Security Force, awarded the rank of second lieutenant, and given the uniform of an officer in the military. Basking in the glow of his new stars, Muhammad decided to honour his new rank in a new way. Surely two brass stars on his epaulettes meant he deserved no less than two wives.

People said that his new, second wife was the one who shined his shoes each morning before he got out of bed. They also said that she would rub his stars with citrus rinds so they would sparkle all day long on her husband's shoulders.

Two years into the life of the PA, Muhammad rose to the rank of colonel, and it was President Arafat himself who pinned the new badges on his sleeves while also bestowing upon him the Legion of Honour, First Degree. Why? Because Muhammad had, with his own personal revolver, executed two men caught collaborating with Israel. It had been a daring operation, one that almost cost Muhammad his life. But that was not all. Muhammad had also rounded up a hundred card-carrying members of Islamist opposition groups. Muhammad had thrown them into Gaza Central Prison and delivered a complete list of their names to the President himself. The first thing Muhammad thought about while coming home from the promotion ceremony was that he would marry two more women. He would marry them at the same time, exactly like the first Muslims used to do. 'A marriage,' he thought to himself, 'to befit my new rank, in accordance with the precepts of Sharia law.'

His two wives—who, like any other two Palestinian factions, knew only envy, jealousy, competition and strife—formed a unity government and began to conspire against Muhammad. Unbeknownst to him, they jointly submitted a single official complaint, demanding that the PA stop 'the wandering-eyed colonel'—which is how they referred to him—from going any further. Arafat called the colonel in and publicly reprimanded him in front of top officials and officers from all the intelligence and security agencies. Arafat raised his voice. 'Why, Muhammad? Why? Look at me. I'm the President and leader of the nation. After spending thirty years married only to the cause, I went and married one woman. How many? One—and only one. So what makes you think you can go and marry four? You think you're better than the rest of us? Is that what you think, Mr. Colonel?' Then Arafat issued a decree prohibiting officers from marrying more than one woman unless they had received special dispensation from the Office of the President. Police officers and intelligence agents agreed to abide by the new regulation, as did all the other branches of the military, though their exact number has never been known by anyone. The policy took effect throughout the entirety of the national territories of the PA, that is the occupied West Bank and Gaza.

As for the man who was so fond of marrying, the new regulation did not stop him daring to challenge the authority of the President. At every gathering, event or meeting he attended, Muhammad would talk loudly to whoever would listen, saying that Arafat wished he could marry more. He never tired of repeating, 'It's not my problem if the President can barely handle one woman. But as for me, I could never be satisfied with just Suha. Being married to one or two isn't enough for me. I swear, if Arafat could, he'd marry ten women— one from each political faction. And then he'd unite the PA and the PLO in a single household.'

*

Walid stood at the corner of the house overlooking the heart of the neighbourhood. He started to watch the sun as it set far, far away, dragging with it the remaining moments of his last day in Gaza until it, and those moments, disappeared behind the yellow sand dunes. He imagined that there the sun would rest its head on the horizon's edge before it slipped, sleeping, into the sea—and then the features of the camp began to dissolve into the spreading twilight.

The lights in the city streets came on suddenly, as if they had just woken from an afternoon nap that had stretched on too long. With each light, the shadows of the place also awoke, as did everything else that sprang to life when light bulbs flickered on.

Walid wandered along until he got to the corner across from Jaber Rayyan's shop. He stood there under the utility pole, where he had arranged to meet his cousin Said.

Walid began to study the stars and constellations with sudden astonishment. High in the distant sky he saw a silver glow amidst the stars of Ursula Minor, and right there in the middle he could make out the features of his father's face. Then he heard the words, 'Your father's been vindicated.' Looking into the night sky, Walid remembered the day his mother said those very words.

Umm Walid was in the middle of sweeping the courtyard with palm fronds when Walid's grandfather, Nimr, walked in and broke the news that Walid's father had been declared innocent. He told her how the police had detained the director of the distribution centre, Khamis al-Sawafiri, and formally charged him with stealing bundles of clothing. Unable to deny it, Khamis had admitted the crime. On top of that, they accused him of conspiring with some of his employees in loading trucks with pilfered bags of flour that were sold to merchant friends of his in Gaza City market.

Umm Walid exploded with a song that rent the heavens. Walid was down the street playing with friends when he heard it. His mother's ululation was like no one else's. She was the only woman in the camp to split her trill into four heaping portions—which she never served at the same time.

Walid ran off to follow the singing that led him back home. When he got there, he found his mother leaning up against the front door with her hands held up high in supplication. Her arms were stretched wide to receive the neighbours, who flocked to congratulate her.

Walid threw himself into his mother's arms and hugged her with all his might, kissing her forehead and hands. She held him tightly, her face drowning in tears of joy.

'Hi, Walid. You're right on time!'

The surprise of hearing his cousin's voice brought Walid back to the moment. No sooner had he replied to Said's greeting than Fawzi Ashour also arrived.

*

Fawzi was short and slightly stocky. He had a delicate face, as round as a Valencia orange and as ruddy as an Anatolian apple. He may have worked as a weaver on a manual loom, but his daydreams took him on journeys far from the din of the textile factory. And unlike his loom, his dreams were woven by electricity. He dreamed that one day he would inherit Marlon Brando's throne in the sultanate of cinema. He would raise his thick right hand in the air and solemnly swear that if they had cast him in *Julius Caesar*, he would have delivered a performance as good as Brando's.

Fawzi would sometimes stumble and fall from the heights of Hollywood into the depths of Cairo's B studios. Fawzi was mad about cinema. When Fawzi impersonated Shukri Sirhan playing Said Mahran in *The*

Thief and the Dogs, he would completely disappear into character. Fawzi often played Sirhan playing Mahran for his friends. And when he did, Said would leap up and threaten Fawzi, his hand clenched in the shape of a revolver. 'Said Mahran, come out with your hands up!'

The three friends would sit and smoke to the rhythm of Said's off-colour epics. Said told the story of Samira Doughan and how she would leave the window to her bedroom open at night for Ibrahim Harb, the Arabic teacher at Mustafa Hafez Boys Elementary. Knowing this, Ibrahim would steal into the side yard and deliver a love letter to Samira. Said told his friends about the rose that Ibrahim had left at her window one night— the same damask rose that caused so much whispering in the neighbourhood. 'She wore that rose in her hair,' Said went on, 'for an entire month. And somehow, as long as it was in her hair, it stayed as fresh as the day Ibrahim first gave it to her.'

Fawzi added, 'I swear to God—anyone who walks by the Doughan house today can still smell that rose.' And he sniffed at the air with nostrils that would not recognize the attar of a rose if they smelled it.

Before he finished the story of Samira, the three friends had agreed on one thing: that her father, Hajj Omar Doughan, would kill her with a rusty knife if he found out what half the camp already knew. He might just do to her what Mahmud Abu Hayya had done to his sister Marwa.

Walid interjected that the two situations could not

be more different. 'When Mahmud killed Marwa, it was out in the open and in front of witnesses. And it was to redeem his family's honour. She deserved it, but Samira does not. It'd be enough to slap her face a couple of times. A few lashes on her back, and she'll repent and never do it again.'

Sheikh Mu'min Abdel Aal happened by just then, his glorious robes flowing as he went. The sheikh was a judge in the Sharia courts and was on his way home after praying at the nearby mosque. A half-stifled laugh escaped from Said and Fawzi. The sheikh cleared his throat, drawing their attention to the greeting that he had uttered and which, still hanging in the air, demanded the courtesy of a reply. Shamed, the three called back with even more elaborate greetings. But as soon as the sheikh was gone, Said began to cackle and howl. 'Yes, sir, Mr. Judge, Mr. Sheikh, Mr. Azhari! Let's have it—that's how men of religion should be!'

'What's so funny, Said?' Walid asked.

'You mean you don't know what the sheikh did? You've always been such a good little boy!'

With a wicked smile, Fawzi butted in. 'Listen to what Said's about to tell you. It all happened while you were in Egypt—I'm sure you haven't heard it yet.'

Then Said began to narrate what they called 'The Tale of the Sheikh'. 'Sabha al-Farran slept with Ali Wafi in his family's place. She lost her virginity to Ali that night and then ran out of the house in such a hurry that she forgot her knickers. She thought about going back to get them, but got scared she'd get caught doing it and then everyone would know.'

Fawzi objected, 'Are we sure that Sabha even wears panties?'

That pissed Walid off. 'You two have no shame. These are people's reputations you're talking about!'

Said ignored Walid's comment and turned to ask Fawzi, 'So, how do you know that Sabha doesn't wear panties? Huh? Fess up! Have you, fine sir, had the good fortune to disrobe the fair maiden in question?'

For a moment, a lascivious smile hung on Fawzi's fine, delicate lips. Then, wryly, he said, 'No, sir. I use logic. Simple logic, nothing more. Consider these facts. Sabha comes from a dirt-poor family. Her father doesn't have a penny to his name. Were she to die, the man wouldn't be able to afford to bury her in a panty-sized shroud. He couldn't even do that for Umm Sabha, even though he sleeps with the old woman every night. Thus, I aver that the Farrans are a family that wears no underpants.'

Said continued his story, ignoring Walid's anger and Fawzi's sarcastic interjections. 'A few days later, Sabha ran off. She'd told her mother what had happened—and now her father was determined to marry her to her cousin Yasser. Sabha refused the marriage, fearing that her cousin would figure out that she wasn't a virgin. She made up a story about wanting to wait until she'd finished high school. Her father stubbornly insisted on going forward with the wedding arrangements, and told the girl that he and his brother, the lucky groom's father, had already agreed all the details. It was at that point that she ran away to the home of sheikh Mu'min Abdel Aal. There, she went on and on telling stories and pleading with the old man, 'Have mercy on me, sheikh! Protect me! My family wants to marry me off to my cousin by force, but I won't consent to it. I'm scared they might come after me and kill me!'

Finally, Said began to talk about the role the sheikh had played in the tale. 'May God grant that noble gentleman a long, prosperous life and reward him for the principled stand he took while he considered that poor girl's plight! Even though that man had no daughters of his own, he took Sabha into his bosom like any loving father would do. Then the good sheikh convinced Sabha's parents to let her remain in his household long enough for him to convince her to change her mind.

'She took refuge in his home. Long-term refuge—it went on for more than three months. At which point, Sabha began to show signs of being pregnant. No one could figure out who the father was. It could have been Ali—he was the one who had first blazed the trail. But it also could have been the Azhari sheikh's—there's no doubt that of late, the industrious man had widened the road somewhat.

'No one believed the torrent of gossip that spilled through the alleys and streets of the camps and city. No one believed all the chatter about the sheikh and Sabha until the day the sheikh announced—four months after she'd taken refuge in his home—that the two of them were legally married. And this made everyone—his family, her family and everyone else in the city and its camps—face the fact that Sabha had become this man's wife fair and square.

'The sheikh said it would be a pragmatic solution to Sabha's problem, in addition to being a highly commendable legal resolution. Not even the girl's father could object.'

After feasting for months on the story of Sabha and Ali, people began to view the story in a different light and began to sympathize with the sheikh, who had done nothing more than use religious dogma to smooth over the bumps in the road. Whenever his name came up, people would say, 'God really owes him one.'

The lights of the city turned off before Said's tongue stopped wagging. The three friends did not stop talking until Walid reminded them that he was travelling in the morning and had to get up early. It was midnight and the outlines of the streets and alleys had faded into the gloom around them. Only then did they say goodnight and goodbye. Only then did each go off, bleary eyed, in the dark, toward his home.

*

The next morning, after performing dawn prayers, Walid quickly ate the breakfast his mother had prepared for him. He kissed his nine-year-old sister, Raja, and said goodbye to her. He picked up his leather suitcase and went out. His mother went with him to where the taxi was waiting. He put his bag in the boot then turned to his mother and embraced her. The car went off with him in it, but his eyes remained glued to his mother. Her face leapt back and forth in the rear view window, and then got smaller. The shawl she held in her fingers billowed and flapped like a flag in the wind. And then her image disappeared in the distance. Nothing remained but the last words she said to him. They rang in his ears, 'Go and come back safe.'

Over the Sinai the train carried Walid to Cairo. He travelled in the third-class carriage for nine tedious hours, six of them choked with the dust of the desert.

That was the last time he would take that trip in either direction. He never made it back to Gaza after that.

Tomorrow, he comes home.

Return

1

I throw my little backpack into the overhead bin and take my seat. Row 19. Seat B. British Airways Flight 153, from London Heathrow to Tel Aviv. The plane is supposed to arrive at 7 am local time. I am no longer thinking about how anxious my mother is, nor about how sceptical she was, doubting I would really come. Her feelings had already begun to change into a kind of waiting whose hours were dissolving now, tonight. By now, on this last night of waiting, she must have surrendered to a sleep as restless as her feelings.

It is 11:15 pm, which makes it 1:15 am in Palestine. 'Believe it, Mama,' I will tell her as I hold her in my arms tomorrow morning, seeking my childhood somewhere in her embrace. 'Here I am, I made it.' And then we will sit down at the squat table to eat. Passengers in my aisle walk right by, taking their seats one by one. Others in the aisle opposite look for their seats there.

I study the passengers as they go by, nervous about which one will be sitting next to me. Their faces flip by like the pages of a book written in different languages and different alphabets. One of these faces belongs to my seatmate, who in all likelihood will be Jewish. Everything points to this likelihood—all the conversations, whispers and thoughts I have overheard since boarding.

I will ignore the issue and my seatmate too. I lean back into my seat and surrender to the half-dozing wakefulness of flying. I might watch a movie once the airplane reaches cruising altitude. I could read the book I brought, Yann Queffélec's novel, *Cruel Weddings*. I finished the first hundred pages yesterday, following the strange story of Ludo, cast into the world by the cruel thrusting of the American sailors who raped his mother. After this great and celebrated American victory, Ludo's mother looks at him and sees only the wrong done her. She rejects him as if he belonged to a complete stranger.

Next to the novel in my backpack is the statuette of Nefertiti, bought so long ago in a souvenir shop in Khan El-Khalili. Today, she travels with me to the friend I bought her for. But I do not reach for the novel, nor for Nefertiti. I might pick up my book later. If someone sits down and wants to talk, I will have to excuse myself from Ludo's company for a while. But if someone asks me where I am from, I will pick up the book and start reading. Even now, I have no idea how I will respond to that question, should it be asked.

It makes me more and more nervous to think about it. *Really, where am I from?*

It is my first trip to Israel. It is the first time I have been on an airplane where all the passengers, or at least most of them, are Jewish. Only once did someone ask me that question before. It happened on the Underground, during my usual rush-hour commute to work in central London.

I was on the Piccadilly line, heading toward Cockfosters, when the man got on at Acton Town. He was about seventy, with an old yarmulke and long curly sidelocks. He wore black trousers, a bright white shirt and an overcoat, even though it was summer. The man smiled at no one in particular, then made a bee-line for the seat next to mine Before the train had even left the station, my neighbour began to read aloud from a book that lay open in his hands. The murmurs and whispers streaming from his lips were surprisingly strident. Unlike Qu'ran reciters who rock side-to-side when they read, this man rocked back and forth.

At first, I did not pay much attention to him. Nor did I read any sign of annoyance on the faces of the other passengers who were, I suspect, busy thinking about other things. No one complained or said a word about the man or his mumblings. No one paid him any mind until he stomped his foot so hard it shook the floor of the carriage. Then he did it again and people began to exchange startled looks. Eyebrows went up and eyes rolled.

Finally, my curiosity got the better of me and I turned to look at my neighbour. He continued to stomp on the floor to the same slow syncopated beat while he went on reading and rocking back and forth, like a clock striking midnight.

All of a sudden, the man stopped reading and his foot stopped stomping. He looked around at us as if our faces would tell him why we were so surprised. His gaze eventually settled on me. He stared, and then glared at me in genuine astonishment.

'Israeli, no?'

I shook my head.

Without relinquishing the look of surprise on his face, he smiled. 'Jew?' He did not wait for me to answer but put his index finger on a line in his book. He began to read the words beneath his finger as it crept across the page.

I gently touched his wrist to stop him and said, 'I'm sorry, sir. I don't speak Hebrew very well.'

My words made the man even more curious. And when I told him the same thing in correct Hebrew, my apology came across like an outright lie. That is how it always is whenever we try to apologize for not speaking a language by using the right words in the language itself.

That only encouraged my neighbour to go on with his questions. 'Egyptian, huh?' he asked in Hebrew.

I shook my head again. *Maybe he thinks the Camp David Accords have somehow made the Egyptians learn Hebrew?*

Then he turned to look at me squarely. 'So where are you from then?'

I decided to put an end to his confusion. 'I'm Palestinian.'

With the innocence of a child and the wonder of a sage, he called out in Hebrew, 'You are a Philistine? A Palestinian?'

Then he began to rattle on in Hebrew. With some difficulty I was able to grasp this: he was on his way to meet his son and go to synagogue. He promised to pray for both of us, because he loved Palestinians and hated war.

When the train stopped at Green Park, the man closed his book and leapt energetically for the door. Before he stepped off, he turned to look at me with a huge, genuine smile on his face. 'Shalom!'

'Salam!' I called back.

A heavy-set man comes walking down the aisle. The shaggy red beard on his face makes him look like my grandfather's old goat. The man goes on toward the rear of the plane. A woman about his age approaches. She is wearing jeans and a light blue blouse, unbuttoned low. In her cleavage, a little Star of David glitters and gleams. She also walks back toward the rear.

Suddenly, a black man in his twenties appears. He looks like a Falasha. I imagine his family emigrating from Ethiopia as part of the airlift between 1984 and 1991. Maybe via Sudan, part of the secret deal with Numeiri. I really don't want him to sit next to me. I do not want to spend these next five hours sitting next to someone like him, with the two of us poring over every moment of Middle Eastern history together. The guy walks by, and I begin to relax.

The next one up in the line slowly creeping toward the back is an old lady. If this woman sits next to me, it won't be any fun at all. But, at the same time, it won't be so annoy—

My thoughts are interrupted by shouts from among the seats on the other aisle. *'Rotza leshevet po, Ima!'* A little girl's voice shrieks, 'I want to sit here, Mama!' I cannot see the girl from where I am sitting, nor the mother, who tries to explain to the girl that the seat she wants is not hers. *'Ze lo hakiseh shelakh!'* The girl screeches out over and over, 'But I want to sit here, but I want to sit here!' I now can hear two small fists pounding on a seat, as she bawls, *'Rotza leshevet! Rotza leshevet!'*

As the stewardess tries to resolve the problem, I go back to watching the passengers as they shuffle by. Some I hope will sit next to me. Some I hope will not. I imagine that I am the one who decides who will sit where, what they should look like, and even what opinions they are allowed and not allowed to have.

A woman in her sixties appears, walks toward me, then walks past. A young North African man reads the seat numbers above my head and makes me nervous. Then he walks on, making way for a large man in his fifties. Another man approaches, panting and out of breath, like he is lugging around a body that belongs to someone else. He is carrying a black book and putting on a pair of thick glasses. I watch him carefully as he sits down in the seat directly across the aisle from me in the middle row. When I realize what sort of book he is reading, I say to myself, *Please God, don't let him stomp his feet when he reads!*

A seventy-year-old woman comes up and stops right next to me, but she does not look up at the seat numbers overhead. Suddenly a beautiful blonde appears right behind her. Her arrival makes me reconsider the calculations I have been making.

I hope she sits next to me. The words repeat in my mind like a mantra. I couldn't care less about the kinds of questions she is probably going to toss at me. Flinging my fear to the wind, I decide I am ready to go to hell itself, as long as I get to sit next to her.

I struggle to get a better look at the woman and notice that she is desperate to find her seat and is not going to wait for the old lady to clear the aisle. She is in such a hurry that she leans over the old lady. Like a lover late for an assignation, she murmurs, 'Excuse me, sir—is this row 19?'

'Yes, miss. No one is sitting in A. Is that what you're looking for?'

The old lady walks past and the aisle opens up to reveal a pair of bare legs. She is not wearing much on top either. She is courteous when she asks to squeeze by me. *My seatmate. Lucky you, Walid!*

I stand up to let her through, not yet believing my good fortune. This blonde is going to be my companion through the depths of the night. She will drift off beside me and I will wake her up at dawn so we can watch the sunrise together. I will even exchange pleasantries in Hebrew with her, if she wants. *'Boker tov, adona!'* ... *'Boker tov, adon!'*

Why is this woman in such a hurry to sit down? Did they seat her next to me deliberately?

The more I think about it, the more paranoid it makes me. At the check-in desk, the attendant took my passport and looked at it. She did not even attempt to disguise her uneasiness. 'I'm sorry, sir,' she told me. 'There's been a mistake with your reservation. The plane is overbooked.'

'How is that my problem? I made my reservation three weeks ago.' That's all I actually said, even though what I really wanted to tell her was that I had been waiting decades to take this trip. I never had the chance to say this because she immediately began to tell me how sorry she was. British Airways would assume all responsibility. She would try to find a prompt solution for my problem. I should relax and not worry, if they could not find me a seat on this plane, they would find me one on the next flight.

'When would that be?'

'Sorry. We will let you know as soon as we have more information.'

Then she stood up and walked away. The whole time she was away, my passport and boarding pass sat on the desk.

A young male attendant came and sat down in her place. He flipped through the pages of my passport, then put it back down and began to help others. Whatever the problem was, it was mine and mine alone.

The first attendant came back and whispered some words in the ear of her co-worker. The man giggled, then the two of them went back to doing their work.

What happened while I was checking in? Did someone in the back room arrange to have this particular woman sit in the seat next to me?

These doubts and suspicions begin to drive me crazy. There is nothing in this world as disturbing to me as my own thoughts. My seatmate is a honeytrap. I will be under surveillance every minute I am with her on this flight. I am sure she has been well trained in how to gather information from subjects like me. And after we land, other agents will step in and take her place.

What a load of crap—why do I listen to these thoughts? They are ridiculous. I am not important in the slightest. Why would Mossad want to keep tabs on me? I am neither a Naguib Mahfouz nor a Palestinian politico from one of the factions. I am not even an activist whose pacifism would be troubling to anybody. I am just a harmless journalist, like hundreds of others.

But what if someone made a mistake? Like what happened to that Moroccan busboy, Ahmed Bouchiki, killed in Norway by a Mossad team who thought he was a Palestinian operative. Bouchiki's murder was a case of mistaken identity. With me, there will be no such mistake. I am a passenger on a plane. As soon as we land, I will walk straight to airport security on my own two feet. There, they will not be able to make a mistake—not even an honest one—even if they wanted to. There's nothing false about my citizenship or my papers. The worst they can do is detain me.

The thought calms me. For a few seconds at least. Then I notice I am looking straight down at the chiselled legs of my seatmate as she squeezes into her seat. The bare skin seems to wink back at me. A reasonable dread comes over me when I imagine that my seatmate's politics could well be Likud, maybe even to the right of Sharon himself.

Just thinking about all this gets me down. I wish I could be rid of all these thoughts passing through my mind. It is just a plane ride.

2

The plane takes off. My homecoming jerks into motion as the engines roar with thunder and the aircraft shakes terribly as it ploughs through the air. The whole cabin is silent until the captain announces that the plane has reached a cruising altitude of almost thirty thousand feet.

When the seatbelt sign goes off, I hear a wave of clicking sounds and sighs of relief. One of the stewards welcomes the passengers on board, and it occurs to me that it is not so different from the recorded announcements you hear on the London Underground: 'Now leaving this station! Next stop, that station! This train terminates at …' It is just as easy to ignore this announcement as it is in the tube. And then I am thinking about my mother. She is sleeping but not sleeping as morning creeps slowly toward her. I am sure she is in bed, but I also know that tonight she cannot sleep.

A year after my father died, my father's sister, Sofia, told her, 'Listen Umm Walid, my girl. Your husband, God have mercy on his soul, has been dead for a year now. You're still young and pretty and—'

'Don't say another word, cousin! After Abu Walid, I can never marry again.' My father's sister swallowed the rest of her words. After that, she never brought up the subject of marriage again.

My mother was young when my father died, not even thirty. She was tall and slim. Her skin was light, and her cheeks were as red as apples. Her button nose was just as small as it was on the day she was born. And her lips were delicate. Even more striking than her beautiful face was her rebellious black hair—no headscarf could ever contain it.

My aunt was not the only one to bring up the subject. My father's father, Nimr, could not stand the thought of my beautiful mother remaining a widow either. Together, the two of them would worry about what people might say if she never remarried. But my mother would not give up her attachment to my father. My grandfather told my mother one evening, 'Listen, daughter: Ahmad was my son. He was the apple of my eye. He was as dear to me as he was to you—even more so. But what happened happened, and by God's decree. And who am I to reject God's wisdom? Besides, you're still young and—'

My mother interrupted her father-in-law with a severity he'd never witnessed before. 'Say no more, please. I'm neither young nor old. I've got a boy who's becoming a man, and a girl. And I want to raise them. I said it when Ahmad died. And I said it again after a year had passed. And now I am repeating it to your face so you never ask me again: *Abu Walid, you are gone, but there will be no other man for me.*' And with this, she closed the file on an idea whose very premise pained her sense of dignity. Sure enough, my mother never remarried. She lived only for my sister and me.

In March 1967, I returned to finish my studies at the university, hoping to return with a degree in hand. My mother always thought that a Cairene girl would snatch me away from her, that I would come back holding a marriage licence instead of a diploma. But the war broke out just days after we finished our final exams. Israel occupied Gaza and Sinai, the West Bank and the Golan. And I never got to go back.

Years later, my sister, Raja, married a relative of ours who was working for a company in Qatar, and she moved there to be with him. So our mother was left to live alone. She saw Raja and her husband once a year, when they came on their summer visit to Gaza. My mother found some consolation in that.

Raja died last year in Qatar. She'd been sick—uterine cancer. And now my mother was doomed to live in total isolation till the end of her days, or so she thought.

I look around. Some of the other passengers are busy reading books. Others are watching videos. Some have turned off their overhead lights and gone to sleep. Or they are pretending to sleep. Meanwhile, the jet engines roar and spit with a rhythm so soft and regular you barely notice it.

Suddenly, the silence is broken by loud snoring. I turn and look around, to see a large man sitting in the aisle seat of the middle section in the row behind us—head on chest, his mouth a heaving hole. His lower lip trembles as he snores, in and out.

The sound rattles my seatmate. She turns to me and asks, 'What the hell is that?' As if she thought I was the one making all the racket.

'Snorting, coming from someone behind us.'

'It's really disgusting, whatever it is.'

But I do not open my mouth to say another word. I just realized I said 'snorting' instead of 'snoring.' I am lost in translation. My words are embarrassed by me, and I by them. By the time I return to Khan Yunis in my mind, the snoring has stopped and my seatmate has gone back to sleep.

'Abu Hatem—listen, cousin. My mother is insisting I stay with my other cousins up in Jabalia Camp. She told me they've fixed up a room in Shafiq's apartment. She says the place is still completely empty apart from the room he furnished for when he gets married. Come and meet me at Beit Hanoun crossing. From there, we'll go to Nasreddine's building, which my mother says is not far from the crossing. That way I'll get to see you right away and then, a few days later, I'll come and stay with you for a couple of days in Khan Yunis before going back up to Jabalia. That way we'll make everybody happy, including my mother.'

'Don't worry about it, cousin. I spoke with your mother and reassured her, we'll do whatever she wants. We don't want to make her unhappy. Whatever you and

she decide on is OK by me. You'll be staying with your cousins and family. I'll come by in the late afternoon and say hello and visit for a while and then go back home. Then I'll come on Thursday at 5 and take you back to Khan Yunis with us. Friday morning, we're going to slaughter a sheep in your honour and right after prayers, we'll put on a feast you'll never forget.'

The sound of the stewardess drags me back from Khan Yunis. She places dinner on my table tray: a vegetable omelette, a piece of feta cheese, four black olives, a slice of tomato and assorted pickles.

My seatmate takes notice and says, 'Yum. Does everyone get one like that?'

'Only if you're a vegetarian.'

I cut the omelette in half and without waiting for her to ask, I say, 'You're welcome to have some of mine. I'm not that hungry.'

She smiles. 'Don't worry about it. I'll eat whatever they bring me.'

I dive into my food and do not repeat the invitation. When her meal arrives, she does the same.

I finish eating and the stewardess comes by to collect the trays. She puts mine on the cart and moves on to the next row. I fold my table tray back up into the seat in front of me. A few minutes later, my seatmate finishes hers and does the same. I lean back into my seat and close my eyes.

Some time later, I am woken by the whisper of soft sobbing. I look over at my neighbour. She has covered her head with her hands and is quietly crying. She gets a hold of herself, stops, and then bursts into tears again.

Of their own accord, the fingers of my hand reach out toward her, and then I turn to her, as if to shield her sadness from the world. *Why am I doing this? No answer.*

I pat her shoulder gently. 'Are you OK, miss? Do you need any help?'

People try to console each other's sadness in so many different ways. You might try to calm a colleague at work. Or even a stranger who sits down next to you on the train. You might pat their arm or back. You might even hug them. We all need to feel the touch of another person sometimes. Even if that person is a total stranger.

But I'm not her colleague and no mere stranger. I'm the Other, aren't I? I'm that kind of person whose being shakes her whole existence. And hers shakes mine. We're not in a position to console each other. She's Israeli, her accent proves it. No doubt she served in the military. Maybe she did her service in the Occupied Territories. Maybe she has shot at Palestinians. Maybe she played a role in the murder of my cousin, Falah. Maybe she has stood at checkpoints … My seatmate might be all this, or she might not.

My mind begins to spin. I start to have second thoughts about what I am doing. But my hand still rests lightly on the woman's shoulder, as if it belonged there.

My seatmate wipes her tears with the back of her hand. I rush to offer her a Kleenex. She politely refuses it, saying: 'No thank you.'

So what? What's the use of being so polite? She said no, and that's that.

Suddenly a wide smile appears on her lips and my Kleenex disappointment vanishes. I am relieved. *Why?* I take my hand from her shoulder and settle back into my seat. My seatmate bends over to reach something on the floor.

'Would you like some?' She takes a large chocolate bar out of her bag and offers me half.

I ask for only one small square, but she hands me two. I thank her and devour them in two bites, mumbling as I chew: 'Mm. This is good chocolate.' Piece by piece, she eats the rest.

She must be in heaven by now. There are women who receive genuine chemical pleasure from chocolate. They eat it anytime and anywhere, knowing that it will give them an endorphin high. Then there are women who eat chocolate either because they want to do without men or because they must do without men. It could be that my seatmate has just been dumped. Maybe she is missing a man who once filled her world with love. In any case, her sadness totals half a bar of chocolate, no more. Perhaps she will wipe away her sorrows now. She really does look more relaxed now than she did when she first sat down.

'May I have that Kleenex after all, please?'

I give her the same tissue she just refused—and in doing so, her rejectionist stance is banished and so are my hard feelings.

She gently pats the chocolate off her lips. In doing so, she wipes away the rest of her sadness. She places the tissue in the little seat pouch in front of her.

'You know, your British accent is charming.'

She glances at me from the corner of her eye before turning to look at me directly, before I have a chance to say anything.

I laugh, making fun of myself while staring back at her. Her eyes have begun to sparkle. I finally reply, astonished, 'My *British* accent?' *That's odd. She can't really like my English—it's mongrel, made up of lots of odds and ends, none of which have much to do with England. Or is she trying to figure out where I'm from?*

'Um, I don't know. I mean, I like the way you speak. Each letter comes out so pronounced.'

The way I speak? Pronounced? I've never met anyone who liked my accent before. Is she really being sincere when she says she likes it? 'You really like it, huh?'

'Mmm.' As she murmurs, her eyes flash with hesitation. It makes me want to go ahead and talk to her. It makes me want to carry the conversation far away from me—to talk about her and her world.

'You know, when you asked me about the seat number, I was hoping it was going to be yours. I said to myself, I'd be a lucky man if this good-looking blonde sat down next to me.'

'Thank you. What else were you saying to yourself?'

She is not only attractive, she is greedy. 'Well, I was thinking you were probably a model or an actress.'

'I am an actress!' she blurts out with a smile.

As she opens this door onto her world, I breathe another sigh of relief. I want her to keep talking about herself, so I ask, 'So you live in Tel Aviv?'

'Yes, so do my parents.'

'You live with them then?'

'Not at all. Well, in the same neighbourhood as them,' she adds with a laugh. 'They live close to me.'

'Do you live by yourself?'

'I've got a friend who stays with me now and then.' She says nothing for a moment. Then she whispers, like she is telling a secret meant only for me: 'Ehud is waiting for me right now, actually.'

'What does he do?'

'Ehud? He's a basketball star. He plays for Elitzur Ashkelon at the moment.'

'Majdal Asqalan.'

'Pardon?'

'Sorry. I was saying that Ehud must be lucky. You too.'

She smiles. 'He isn't "the one",' she says.

'Oh, no? Does anyone have this honour?'

She pauses and looks away briefly, then back at me. The circle I cracked begins to open wider: unexpectedly, she begins to unfold her story.

'My relationship with Ehud hangs halfway between friendship and love, as if each of us is so terrified of the other that we want to flee in the opposite direction. It is like I only have half a heart, even though each time

I do want to surrender all of it. All my affairs end in midstream. In the middle of the road, halfway there. Why am I like this?'

To my surprise, I am not taken aback by this sudden intimacy, this torrent of very personal details. 'Perhaps you've never experienced true love, or met someone who can keep your heart,' I reply.

She pauses again, for longer this time, then continues: 'Actually, I did have this kind of relationship. A wonderful love. It's the reason I was sad just now. It's the reason I came to London, and it's the reason I am returning, too.'

I lean in closer, listening intently, but all she says is, 'He lived in London. He was from Ukraine.'

'What happened?'

'It ended abruptly …'

'You had a long-distance relationship?'

'Not quite. In fact, I brought him to Tel Aviv.'

'Just like that?'

'Well,' she replies. 'He was Jewish, so …' *She doesn't need to finish the sentence. As a Jewish person, he would have the 'right of return', the right all Palestinian refugees have been denied since the Nakba in 1948.*

I remain quiet, and she continues:

'I was in London on my way back to Tel Aviv after visiting my grandfather in New York. I was spending the night with Sarah, a close friend of mine. She threw a party for me and invited a bunch of her friends. She introduced me to this good-looking guy, who had just got here. For the rest of the night, we never left each other's side. We kept drinking and drinking the marvellous wine that Sarah always serves. And we kept dancing and dancing until dawn, when he and I ended up at his flat in Hammersmith.

'I fell in love with the guy, the moment I met him. After that, we emailed each other constantly. We built a bridge of letters and notes over which we sent all the important data about our lives. A few months later, I went to London to see him. We spent a lovely ten-day holiday there. Ten long summer days together. We went to the cinema a lot. We sat on every barstool, restaurant chair and park bench we could find. We fed the pigeons in Trafalgar Square and the ducks in Hyde Park. We smelled every rose there was to smell, and wandered from one museum and theatre to the next. We went to see *Les Mis* and loved it.

'He took me out to dinner to his favourite restaurant, a Lebanese place on Edgware Road called Al-Dar. He had a close Arab friend from his English night school, who had taken him there once. The food was unbelievably good.'

'I know this restaurant,' I say. 'I like it too.'

She smiles, and continues, 'We were walking to the restaurant and he whispered in my ear: "You Israelis are just like the Arabs. You love your hummus and falafel." I whispered back: "I can't wait to get you to Tel Aviv so I can stuff you with chickpeas!" Then I said, in English and then in Hebrew: "I love you. *Ani aheevat*."

He replied in Russian: "*Ya lyublyu tebya.*" I asked him to say it again, and he went on until I memorized it. "*Ya lyublyu tebya.*" Now we were lovers in three languages. Shortly after that, he moved to Israel.'

A citizen in a land that never belonged to him or to his ancestors, I add silently; while I, who do belong to that land, have remained a refugee for decades.

'But I utterly I failed in my attempt to get him to stay in Israel,' she says. 'I could not hold onto him, even though I personally brought him over from London. I stood by his side through thick and thin, throughout his time in Israel. I helped him escape the worst mess of all, when he found himself floundering about in the face of the Intifada that had begun to explode in the territories.'

I nod, thinking of the soldiers who refuse to serve in the occupied West Bank and Gaza, and call them by their name: 'You know, I like this guy. He reminds me of the refuseniks …'

She looks at me and stops speaking, and then becomes lost in thought for a time without replying. Then, just like that, she throws herself into the world of cinema and acting, trying to change the whole subject as if seeking refuge there. She begins with an anecdote about being at the Eilat Film Festival with 'other Israeli celebrities' two years earlier: 'It was risky for me even to participate, because it opened right as the war was starting against Saddam Hussein, and Iraq was all everyone wanted to talk about. The people in Eilat were surprised that we showed up at all, and then they made fun of us, saying that the only reason we came to Eilat was to escape from Tel Aviv before Saddam's missiles came down!'

My seatmate goes on talking as if we come from the same country. As if we share the same fears, the same constellations of film stars. As she recounts stories about the festival, my mind recalls televised scenes of the war—the live coverage of American attacks that sowed democracy across Iraq. The tonnes of ordnance that went into ploughing deep furrows across the burning old fields of despotism.

I let her talk and wander off in my mind to Asqalan, where her boyfriend plays basketball. Majdal Asqalan is where the protagonist of my novel is from. His whole family is from there. If he, Adel El-Bashity could hear what she is saying, he would shout: 'If only our conflict took place in stadiums! If only the shots fired were at goals, not on people, we would have already founded a Democratic State of Football that stretched from the Mediterranean to the Jordan River, and there would be enough room for all footballers to live there in peace and harmony!' Sometimes Adel's optimism seems ridiculous to me, and it makes me chuckle to imagine that even football could peacefully coexist between the two sides in the foreseeable future. It would be more like El Salvador and Honduras in the 1969 World Cup qualifiers—when football led to war.

She stops talking, and I don't want to interrupt the silence. But she turns to me though realizing only now that she has gone on too long or shared too much. Coyly, she asks, 'I'm sorry—where did you say you were from?'

3

The question surprises me. From the moment I sat down in my seat until the moment she asks the question, it has been bothering me. At first I am nervous, too unsettled to choose an answer. I could say, for instance, that I am Greek or Cypriot or Lebanese, or anything. I could pick any other nationality—anything but Palestinian. I am afraid someone might overhear and shout out: 'Palestinian! This man's a Palestinian!' What if someone got up and made a public announcement, 'Ladies and gentlemen: please be advised that there is a Palestinian on board!'

If this had been my seatmate's first question, I might not have answered it. But now, after getting to know each other, I am not in a position to ignore her. Whatever apprehensions I may have, they belong to the past. Still, I decide to play dumb. 'Where am I from? You never asked.'

'No, I've asked you twice now.' And then wryly, she repeats it again.

'I'm Palestinian. I have British citizenship, but I am Palestinian.'

'Aha. A Palestinian, huh?' she says. It is as if I had tried to put one over on her, or my answer is not good enough. She plays with a strand of her hair. Under the faint overhead light, it has lost most of its golden sheen.

Flatly, even coldly now, she asks, 'Are you taking a tour of Israel?'

'No, I'm visiting family in Gaza.'

'Gaza?' She actually gasps as she says it.

'Yes. Gaza.'

She stops playing with her hair and turns toward the window to hide her reaction. She rests her chin on her hand and stares out. The window has now turned into a small black mirror that casts shadows over things we may think but cannot see. All around us the jet engines hum in a din so constant it sounds like nothing.

My seatmate turns away from her mirror and asks in a trembling voice: 'Do you often visit Gaza?'

'Not at all. This will be my first trip in thirty-eight years. The truth is that I haven't seen my mother in that long.'

She bolts upright in her seat. 'My God! Thirty-eight years! How have you managed to stay away from your mother and family all these years? You're not a negligent son, are you? You don't look cruel, but ... I'm sorry for your mother.'

'The occupation is what's cruel. Not me ...'

She does not comment. I begin to rattle on as my bitterness gets the better of me, 'I haven't been able to go back since 1967. I wasn't allowed to go back.'

'Of course, of course. I hadn't thought of that. I'm really sorry. It hadn't occurred to me that you were unable to visit ... Gaza, huh?'

'Yes. I'm going there with my new British passport. I just got it. Without it, I couldn't go via Tel Aviv.'

For some unknown reason, I begin to tell her my life story. She listens with interest and curiosity. She watches me without interrupting or saying a word, her head propped in the gap between our seats. She studies me as if I were spinning a fantastic yarn.

'I was born in 1948, in Asdud. In the place you now call Ashdod. My family left during the war, we went to Gaza, along with so many others from southern Palestine. We fled there and settled. I spent my childhood and youth in the camps of Khan Yunis. I was educated in Gaza all through secondary school. When I finished, I went to study at Cairo University. After graduating, I wandered the world, a refugee standing on his own two feet—though one was made of exodus without end, and the other a journey without destination. I collected my exiles one by one, and labelled them according to the numbers of years I lived in each. I watch history in our part of the world and notice that it weighs our existence on a broken scale. For every Jewish immigrant to Israel, a dozen Palestinians are driven out.' Then I add: 'If it seems lopsided, it's because the scale that measures us has never been balanced.'

My seatmate takes refuge in silence. She does not put up any resistance to my last attack, which, in any case, was not one I had planned to make. Instead, she sends whatever anxiety she is feeling out into the night sky. She studies herself in the blank mirror. At the same time, her hand creeps over and gently clasps mine.

Returning from her distant musings, she twists to face me. Her fingers send warmth across my hand. 'I hope you have no delays in seeing your mother and that you have a good time together. I hope that there can be peace between us and the Palestinians. We're tired of the situation, all of us. The problem is not the people, it's the politicians. Our politicians and yours. Sharon doesn't want peace, nor does Arafat.'

As she speaks, she retracts her hand and shifts her weight onto the forearm that rests between our seats.

The extremists on your side and the extremists on ours. They always say that when they want to parse the crime and reapportion blame for the shedding of Palestinian blood. Your extremists and our extremists. Fine. I'd love to answer her with a simple quote from Mahmoud Darwish: get out. Leave our lands. Evacuate our territories and quit our sea. Get out of our wheat, our salt, our wounds. Leave the vocabulary of our memory. Then—and only then—can you take care of your extremists while we take care of ours.

I say none of this to her. What is the use of dredging up the entire Middle Eastern conflict in a fleeting meeting between two strangers sitting next to each other on a flight? When I do talk, I say something else entirely: I tell her that I hope Palestinians and Israelis might leave the battlefield behind them and learn to share a life together. I hope that one day she and I might walk together along a long road with no checkpoints between us. No assassinations and no suicide bombers, no soldiers and no militants, no Zionism and no Palestinian national liberation, no Intifadas and no settlements, no Sharons and no Arafats, no Abu Mazens and no Shaul Mofazes, no warlords, no settlers, no Apache helicopters, no F-16s and no car bombs. I hope that we could be just two regular passengers passing the night on any flight.

After going over the last of my misgivings, I ask: 'By the way, you haven't told me your name yet.'

'My name's Dana. Dana Newman, but my friends call me Dana Ahuva.'

'Dana Beloved. It's got a ring to it. It reminds me of Dana International. Remember him—or, I mean, her?'

Laughing, she comments: 'Yeah. But unlike her, I'm not interested in a sex change.'

Then she turns to me and asks me what my name is.

'Walid Dahman,' I say.

She repeats my name after me, as if she has heard it before, 'Walid. Walid.'

'Do you know me, Ms. Dana?'

Reluctantly, she lets out a laugh, 'Not at all. I'm just listening to the music of your name. Walid.' Each time she murmurs it, she stretches it out. Then she wonders aloud. 'Tell me about yourself, Walid. What do you do?'

She smiles and her clear eyes sparkle. As I respond, she clutches her arms around her chest and listens intently.

'I'm married to an English woman, and we have two boys. I'm a journalist. I work for *Akhbar al-Arab*, it's an international Arabic newspaper out of London. I also write different kinds of things.'

'Like what?'

'I write about politics and culture and the arts. I've published three novels—I'm working on my fourth right now.'

'Have you finished writing it?'

'I'm not happy with the title I've chosen, and I haven't given it a proper conclusion. In any case, I'm going to revise some of the scenes. I might add a number of details.'

Before we get into some kind of 'chat-with-the-author' discussion, I add: 'I've given it a number of titles actually, but I haven't been able to decide on one yet. Here are some: *Via Israel. Land of Transgression. Shadow Homeland. Twenty More Days. The Story of Adel El-Bashity*. I've thought about giving the novel the kind of ending that precludes any sequels. Or the kind of conclusion that looks like the beginning of another. Or the kind of ending that leaves the door open to all sorts of speculation about what just happened or what might happen next. Or maybe I should leave it up to readers to decide how the story ends.'

'I don't understand,' says Dana.

'Of course, of course. I haven't given you a sense of what the novel is about and who the characters are. Luckily, we've got a long night ahead of us ... We're riding in a caravan, suspended in the sky—by pillars of illusion! The best I can do is mention some of the highlights of the book. Just give me a second.'

I get out of my seat and stand in the aisle amidst a chorus of breathing souls. Here and there, I make out whispers amidst the loud sawing of snorers. I swing my arms and legs a bit and take a few steps down the aisle and come back.

'There. That's much better. Let's get back to the story. Do you still want to hear it?'

'Of course I do. Please begin.'

'Adel El-Bashity is a Palestinian with German citizenship. He works in a branch of Deutsche Bank in Frankfurt. He returns to Gaza thirty years after going abroad for his education. He goes via Ben Gurion Airport, then through Erez crossing. When Adel was nineteen, he was in love with the girl next door, Leila Dahman. In reality, she's based on one of my relatives. All the Dahmans in Gaza are related to us. Back when he enrolled in the university in Frankfurt, he'd promised himself that he'd marry no one but Leila. For her part, she promised to wait for him to finish his studies and return. But Adel never did return. The '67 war breaks out and Gaza falls under occupation. He doesn't come back. He decides to continue his studies and gets an MBA.

'Leila's now forty-eight years old. She awakes after a long sleep inside the heart of this man who is just over fifty. And this man's heart now itself awakes after a long sleep and begins to beat again.

'When it becomes possible for Adel to return, he decides to go to Gaza and search for Leila. *We need each other now. There's enough life left in us for this love to last.* These are the words he murmurs to himself the day he walks out of his apartment on his way to Frankfurt airport.

'In the airplane to Tel Aviv, Adel meets Arna Katsoff. She's an Israeli woman in her fifties, a professor of political science at Hebrew University. She tells him that she's just spent a few days in Washington DC, delivering an invited lecture at Georgetown University. Her talk was about the latest developments in the Middle Eastern conflict, and prospects for peace in the region. She'd come to Frankfurt for only a couple of days during which time she'd visited the Jewish Museum and the Judengasse Museum nearby. She came to Frankfurt as part of a programme she'd arranged for herself to visit sites in the history of anti-Jewish persecution.

'Arna tells Adel about what she saw in both museums, and about the life of Jews in the Judengasse, one of the oldest Jewish ghettos in Germany. She talks to Adel about how Frankfurt's Jewish community suffered during the Holocaust. Adel feels that Arna has chosen from the outset to talk to him primarily through the lens of Jewish suffering, even though neither he nor his forefathers had anything to do with this history—except insofar as he and his family, like all other Palestinians, were themselves transformed into its indirect victims. When he speaks to her, he tells her about how the immigration of European Jews created multiple tragedies for Palestinians, tragedies that culminated in the Nakba of 1948, and the expulsion of his family and their relocation to the refugee camps of Gaza, and then again, in the occupation of the rest of Palestine, which has gone on for thirty-eight years.

'Adel and Arna sit next to one another throughout the flight, each of them going over old memories in their own minds. Depressing, sad memories. Unsettling ones, haunted by feelings of fear and apprehension, curiosity and defiance.'

Dana does not seem terribly interested in hearing much more of the tangential story—and she cuts me off. 'Less detail, more plot, please. Does Adel meet Leila?' She punches me on the leg and a man sitting behind us clears his throat loudly to voice his displeasure. Dana lowers her voice now, 'Come on—cut to the chase.'

'I still haven't decided whether Adel and Leila find each other or not. I hope to figure that out while I'm in Gaza. Anyway, that's the general idea of the novel— even though I don't know how I should end it.'

'What's holding you back?'

'Nothing. I just prefer to wait until my trip is over before I write the ending. That way I can develop the second narrative thread my wife suggested, the story of what happens during my trip and what I experience. It might give me an opportunity to talk with my novel's hero about his future with Leila. And together we might figure out an ending that joins the two stories. I usually like to talk to my characters about the basic issues in their lives. And then there's also the possibility that something might surprise me on the trip.'

She looks up at the small lamp above our heads and studies it for a few moments, then turns to me and adds, 'I've got an idea for the title of this novel that's still sitting in the belly of its mother. *One House, Two Shadows*. What do you think?'

'*One House, Two Shadows*. Hmm.'

I pretend to think about her suggestion. My fingers curl around my chin like a director unconvinced by the performance of his actors. She looks at me and I continue, 'Hmm.'

Finally, she cuts me off midstream. 'Listen, in this country you and me are headed to together...' There's a note of nervousness that makes her voice quaver. 'In this country where you and I will separate and go our own ways, there is only one land. Only one place to live, only one house. Even so, when the sun rises over the place and casts its rays across the land, you see two shadows. Walid, you and I are two shadows thrown together in a single place. What happened to my people cast black shadows over yours. What's happened to you makes the shadows over us darker still. We are two peoples who will never be at ease. And whenever things seem to be calming down, they get even worse.'

'One house that has two shadows. It's true. Throughout history, this land was a field for sowing shadow and light. Only in their essential opposition do light and shadow take shape and last. Look at shadow. It's born in light, and it dies in darkness. What a strange, fragile thing: it comes to life as soon as light is born, and disappears when the light dies. Shadow is patient. It's like Job. It bears us and perseveres when it is high noon and our footsteps crush the shadows underfoot. You don't know Job, do you? He's a prophet who, people believe, suffered from flesh-eating worms. Like Alexandrians, Gazans celebrate Job each year by going and swimming in the sea. They believe that Job used to go on a certain Wednesday each year to bathe himself in the sea, knowing that the saltwater would heal his burning wounds, and cleanse his body for an entire year.

'You know, after marrying my father, my mother did not get pregnant for a whole year. She was a young girl. Thirteen. The women in Asdud told her to bathe in the sea on Job Wednesday. They told her to be like the Virgin Mary and give herself to the first wave that crashed over her body. They told her to sing a little song seven times to the sea while she was doing this:

Oh Sea, Oh Wave-maker,
Fill my belly with a little one,
My husband will divorce me,
If I don't bring him a son!

'You're laughing! You're going to laugh even more when I tell you my mother began to doubt whether the sea really had answered her prayer and made her pregnant with me. Once she tried to test her strange hypothesis, and began to tell my father, 'You know, Abu Walid, it's not impossible that the sea impregnated me.' My father laughed and said: 'You really are crazy! You believed those women—you thought you were the Virgin Mary? If the sea had impregnated you, wouldn't Walid's eyes be blue?' My mother was stunned. She was holding me in her arms and looked down at my eyes, then said: "You're right, Abu Walid. This boy's eyes are as black as the night." It'd make my mother and father laugh whenever they remembered that.'

Now Dana and I are laughing about it too. She turns to me and, searching for the blackness of the night in my eyes, says: 'You people have some strange traditions.'

'Dana, our country is bursting with history and languages and war, magic and facts and fables, prophets and saints and liars and sinners. And together, all these things have created a great human tradition. On top of this, they've also created a long chain of catastrophe and ruin. I do like the title you're proposing for my novel. I thank you for giving it to me. It turns out you're a novelist too.'

'And you're a philosopher. By the way, if I ever marry and can't get pregnant, I'll head to the sea in Tel Aviv on a Wednesday, just like your mother did. I'll swim in the sea in the early morning and again at sunset so I can have twins. But let's talk about you, not your book.'

'OK. I've lived in London for about eleven years. I hate violence in any form.' *If I were in charge of recruiting for Mossad, I would reject Dana without a second thought, even though clearly she'd have no problem getting the enemy to fall for her.*

'I love life and people and peace. But tell me—'

'Yes?'

'If I asked you to send me something you've written, would you? Would you send some of your writing to an Israeli woman you met on a plane?'

'Only if you admit—'

But before I can tell her what I want, we are interrupted by a stewardess. 'Would either of you like a glass of water?'

We answer with one voice: 'Thanks.' And then we forget what it was we were talking about, and our confessions hang in the air like unspoken confusion.

I take a pen and piece of paper out of my trouser pocket, and ask her to write down her email address. She does not hesitate. I take the paper from her hand and rip off the bottom corner. I write my email address on it and give it to her. She looks at the paper for a bit, then stuffs it into her little bag. 'I'd love to look at something you've written, and we can write to each other. We might even become friends. Who knows?'

'Good—I'll send you some of what I've translated into English.'

'I promise to write to you, to make sure you arrive in Gaza safely.'

I put the paper back in my pocket. I have no idea whether I really will send her anything, or whether she will really follow through on her promise to write. But in any case, when I go back to writing *One House, Two Shadows*, it will be with a completely different pulse.

This seems like a natural place to end the conversation for a while, but I decide instead to return to the story she had begun to tell, the story that had begun, in fact, with her weeping.

'Dana, if I may ask, you said you had come to London because of your Ukrainian boyfriend. I'm curious: does that mean he moved back?'

She exhales before picking up the story. 'Remember that Lebanese restaurant on Edgware Road? The recommendation from Dani's Arab friend?'

'"Dani" …?'

'Yes. It was the name I gave him when he moved to Israel. "Daniel".'

'"Dani and Dana" …?' I muse.

She continues: 'So, Dani's classmate. They had long conversations about Dani's decision to become an Israeli. He told him: "You'll be another number in the annals of Jewish immigration to Palestine, but you'll never be more than a second-class citizen no matter what you do. You'll be given a house easier than you know. Probably in a settlement built on Palestinian land. You'll do your service in the Israeli army, and only if you're killed or badly wounded will your service come to an end. If you come out all right, you'll remain in the reserves for ever, waiting to be called up for the next war. You'll be thrown into a fight that's not yours at all,

96

or that hasn't been yours until now, at least. Perhaps you'll kill someone or become someone's jailer. Maybe you'll refuse to serve and become a conscientious objector. My friend, making *aliya* is a package deal. You can't choose this or that part and leave the rest behind. You buy it all, you can't haggle, and you can't pay for it in instalments."'

I nod, and say, 'If I was his classmate, I would say the same.'

'And what about me?' she asks.

I don't reply, and she finishes the story: 'Anyway, you're just repeating what he said to me after he had been in Israel for some time, that everything his friend had said was true. He said he was sorry, that our relationship had been based on a deceptive contract. "You brought me to Tel Aviv, to a land I'd never belong to," he said. "You found yourself a lover immigrant. And I went with you, and with you I got Israel. But the deal's off now. I'm cancelling it. I have to go." And he left.'

'Did you meet him after that?'

'Actually, I came to London to convince him to return, to me at least if not to Israel. But it was a "mission impossible". The young Communist was still living inside him. Dani came to London a few years after *perestroika*, when his Jewishness awakened. He searched for himself in London, without success. He fell in love with me, and agreed to join me in Israel in the hope he might find his true self. I don't blame him. He was not born there, his memories are not from there.'

'I am sorry for your loss,' I say. 'But Dani did the right thing.' At this she looks away, then down, then out the window. 'Listen, Dana,' I continue, 'if this land was promised to the Jewish people by your God, as lots of Jewish people say and even believe, what about the Arabs' God? If God exists, He must belong to everyone. He must be just and fair and wise. There's no way God would take the land away from one people in order to give it to another. No God would ever do that. No God would ever don the uniform of a settler and send armies out to kill and oppress. God would never do such a thing, because if He did it would mean He had stooped to our level. I'm sure Dani had reached this conclusion through his experience.'

'I had similar experience to Dani's. Should I leave, too?'

I'm not sure what she means by this, but after a few moments' silence, without really agreeing to, we stop talking. Dana picks up her small headset and covers her ears. She turns off the overhead lamp, and puts her seat back as far as it will go. She adjusts how she is sitting and sinks into the backrest. I realize she wants a bit of rest, some respite from the conversation that remains wide awake in the depths of the night. I follow suit and soon we are both asleep.

At the first moments of dawn, our eyes open to the flashing seatbelts light, and the sound of the stewardess announcing that our plane is preparing to land.

The plane shudders over the sea. The water appears

to rush at us as if it were trying to cover our wheels. Then scattered palm trees begin to throw themselves at us just before the plane shakes one last time as it hits the runway. The aircraft finally begins to slow down like a person trying to catch their breath after a long run. It pivots on the runway and heads toward the gates where it will rest, exhausted after its journey.

4

So this is Palestine. Fifty-seven years after the Nakba I experienced as a child. I have carried the Catastrophe inside me ever since Asdud fell. And now, here I am returning, searching for a piece of Palestinian soil to kiss. But there's nothing here to kiss but a tiled corridor and a terminal hall filled with throngs of passengers. They mill around in front of the passport control booths and pretend they are queuing up.

I take my place in a line and an image comes into my mind—this is right where Leah Portman stood more than two years ago. Or maybe she stood over there. My eyes search for footprints, even though I know there are none. I met Leah at a literary event at the School of Oriental and African Studies more than a year ago, when she gave a talk about her first visit to Israel and Palestine. About three months ago I called her and told her I was thinking about visiting Israel on my way to Palestine.

'I'll be there at the same time,' she exclaimed. 'I'm going to visit my sister who lives in Israel.' I proposed that we travel together, and she was enthusiastic, 'Great idea, let's do it.'

I suddenly expanded my invitation, 'Would you take me to Israel and be my friend and translator? I'll take you to Gaza to meet my mother.' *Would I have really done that? I can picture myself, introducing her to my mother and the rest of my family, 'This is Leah, Leah Portman, a Jewish woman from Britain who's a friend of mine.' They would go insane! First of all, they would absolutely refuse to accept that we were just friends—platonic friends. Then they'd start to beat the drums of scandal against me, their so-called relative, who after so many years, comes back home with a woman who is neither wife nor cousin. I can already hear what my cousins would say, 'He comes back with this woman in tow, but that's not all. Noo! He comes with a Jewish woman!' And then the women would start to chime:*

Leah, Leah, little girl,
Blondie, blondie, German curls!
Forty years he's been away,
With a Jew he's back today!

My mother would join right in, crying out, 'What shame! You left and returned in shame, you're going out and doing who knows what with whom! Go send her home before they kill her and get you too.'

Better to follow the advice of the narrator in Samir El-Youssef's novel Pentonville Road, *when the narrators tells Kathy, who visits Gaza without telling anyone what her religion is, 'If you tell them you're a Jew, they'll make mincemeat out of you.'*

I do not really think they would grind up Leah into kofta. No—they would not do that. Samir's narrator exaggerates. The Israeli journalist Amira Hass lived in Gaza for a while, and she was never ground up. On the contrary, she used to hang out with President Arafat and his aides all the time—she was chummy with everybody. Besides, the Dahman family has never hurt anyone before. Most likely, my mother would welcome Leah in her usual way—with open arms. *'We take good care of all our guests, son.'*

Leah laughed into the phone, 'OK Walid, let's do it. Let's go together. I never would have imagined it.'

She called a few days later to tell me that she would have to postpone her trip to Israel because a cultural project in Germany had suddenly come up. So now Leah is returning to Germany, the place from which her parents fled during the Second World War. Her grandparents had been killed in the camps. Her parents made it to England and settled in the Jewish neighbourhoods of north London. Leah was born in London. She was blonde, and the older she got, the more striking her Ashkenazi looks became. Her eyes were blue, and she wore a cap that hid some of her fine blonde hair. She wore loose blouses that looked like Egyptian galabiyyas, and walked like she did not care about anything. I can imagine her standing in one of these lines and saying, 'I'm a British Jew!' It did not matter to her that her sister was Israeli.

Leah was anguished about the moment of her

arrival, just as I am now. She wrote about the experience of arriving in Israel. 'I was already nervous and on edge when I got there. But I was even more disturbed when people told me to bend down and kiss the ground beneath my feet. I couldn't understand why I was supposed to do that. I'm not Israeli, and this land wasn't promised to me. I wasn't making *aliya*, nor would I ever. I was born British and I will always be British.'

She said she did not belong to this land. It was a foreign country to her. Dana, in contrast, is coming back to her own country. She belongs here—this is home. But Adel El-Bashity and me? We used to belong to this place before they did. We belonged to the place and its history, the past and the present, story and fact, light and shadow. Is it really still our home?

My emotions spin around as I stand in line with everyone else. Step by step we creep forward toward the booth, and suddenly a question pops into my mind. *What land will you kiss when you walk out of the airport, Walid? Will you kiss the soil even if it isn't as red as the henna on a peasant girl's hands? Will you kiss it even if the oil of olives no longer courses through its veins? I'm not Dana and I'm not Leah Portman. And the land I'm standing on is no longer Palestine. And the big blue sign on the wall speaks to me exactly like it speaks to any other foreigner: 'Welcome to Ben Gurion Airport.'*

From the moment we land, I look around in astonishment. I see nothing but ordinary people. People are eating breakfast. People are sipping coffee in the beautiful little cafés carefully scattered throughout the terminal so as to entice the weary traveller to sit and stay a while. Are these ordinary people? The question belongs to Adel El-Bashity, but I re-ask it when I find myself in the same situation he was in. And then another question: why did three Japanese gunmen turn the terminal of the old Lod airport into a bloodbath in 1972? Did Palestinians really need Japanese kamikazes to launch a revolution for them? Did they want the Palestinian struggle to emulate their self-destructive example?

Adel El-Bashity laughs cynically. 'Turns out that the roots of Palestinian resistance go back to the kamikazes!' And I whisper back in my protagonist's ear, 'Yes, but look at the contemporary grandchildren of those kamikazes, Adel—not only do they not give a damn, but they can't even do anything right.'

Someone starts shouting in Hebrew—one of the men wearing a broad black hat and sidelocks. A few metres away stands a woman wearing a headscarf, a dark blue blouse and a long grey skirt that goes down all the way to her black shoes. She is clutching a stroller where an infant sleeps. She tries to cut into the line, but someone else stops her. The man tries to persuade the other man to let her in, but he will not budge. They raise their voices as they argue and soon it turns into a shouting match. Eventually the woman retreats, but not before she has handed two passports to the man in the line.

Now it is the man's turn. He goes up to the window

and says a couple things to the security officer and points at the woman. The officer calls out the woman's name, 'Miriam Amar', and she pushes the stroller forward and walks up to the window. As she passes the other man, I notice he looks beaten and tired.

Now it is my turn, the moment I give myself up to an officer who, at some level, works for Israel's Internal Security Agency. Ever more nervous, I drag my feet toward the window not more than two metres in front of me. I put on a brave face and try to hide the noise of my thumping heart. I can barely stop it from flying out of my body and running down the corridor. My chest trembles with each slow step I take. The prospect of being refused entry terrifies me, as does the possibility of being shunted into a side room for interrogation. I picture the officer peeling away my life history layer by layer, wanting to know all there is to know about me.

What if this officer—and she is the real piece of the picture to focus on here—sends me back to London? What then? Everything falls apart. My mother, who dreams of my arrival and who is waiting for me to get there, in an hour or so. Waiting for the joy of her life, this child now fifty-seven years old who is going to walk up to her and hold her in his arms, where she would nurse him on stories she had kept hidden for decades. And my dreams—they too will fall apart. My dreams of retrieving a homeland, which has spread out through the hallways of my life and fed me the bitter taste of separation time and time again.

'Good morning!' I say in an official-sounding voice to the thirty-something woman sitting behind the glass at the booth. She looks at me through prescription glasses as I slip my passport into the slot beneath the glass.

She takes it and replies with the same formal politeness, 'Good morning. How are you today, sir?'

'Fine, just fine.'

She flips through my passport without saying a word. Some time goes by before she gives me a look, then studies my passport again with a puzzled expression. She types a bunch of words into the keyboard while the computer screen turns its back on me. I say nothing as I listen to the clacking of the keys recording my life. *Tiktik. Taka-taka-tak. Tik-tak-tika-tika-tik. Tak.*

The woman bites her lower lip and murmurs, 'Hmm.' A moment later she lets out a long 'Ummm.' Her eyebrows slide upwards across her forehead, forming high arcs over big eyes staring at something in disbelief. All of this makes me very nervous. 'I notice that there's a lot in your file.'

Maybe she only says it to explain all her hemming and hawing and the shock on her face. Maybe she is still forming her decision, a decision that might make my life much more difficult. *She's probably got no choice in the matter: either she'll ask me politely to enter the interrogation room, or, with equal politeness, she'll trick me into going there. Once they're finished, I'll walk out of the room and leave the airport, the same way*

Adel El-Bashity did. That is, only after her colleagues in Shin Bet pound into me the fact they wanted Adel to understand: You are not in Palestine—you are in Israel. Never forget it. *I will not forget it—not even if I had been born on the very land where this airport now sits, not even if they discovered my forefathers' bones buried under this terminal. They will wink and nod at my being British. They'll even tell me how smart it is to be British. They did the same thing to Adel, telling him, 'You should thank the Lord you're German!' And without thinking he replied, 'Even if I held the citizenship of every country in the world, I will never stop being Palestinian.' Even if my memory is made of a past that has no counterpart in the present, this past of mine has the taste of Truth. My country is a fact that has refused to die, even when it was assaulted by history itself. My country isn't a shadow. My country is a split image—part of which can be found here, part of which is over there, with my mother.*

I watch the woman holding my passport, all the while conscious of the fact that she is watching me through the file on her computer screen. *Tik-tik. Taka-taka-tak. Tak-tika-tik.*

The minutes pass slowly. Cold. Heavy. Excruciating. I find myself hoping that she will ask me a question. Just one question. Or that she might say something. Not just these ums and hmms, but an actual, audible word. But she does not—and her silence is torture. She bites on the knuckle of her index finger, then slides it across her teeth. She sighs out loud, and shakes her head in evident confusion. *What shall I do with you? No doubt that's what she's saying to herself right now, as if she wants me to be even more bitter than I am.* She goes back to the keyboard, bites her lips again and lets out another long 'Hmmm', followed by an 'Ummm' that never seems to end.

Now I am still more anxious. When the woman turns to the left and picks up a black telephone, I nearly explode. She dials a number, 'Tik-tik-tak-tak' and puts the receiver to her ear. This woman is calling the person who drags people into the interrogation room. She lets it ring for a few seconds, then puts the receiver down, and sits back in her chair.

What's going on in this woman's mind? Did she have second thoughts about calling the higher-ups in security, or is she playing with me, enjoying the experience of watching me squirm?

'Is this your first visit to Israel?' The question catches me off-guard.

'Yes.'

'What's your address in Israel?'

'I'm going to Gaza.'

'What?'

Her fingers start to type again. She must be recording everything I am saying. So I add, 'I haven't seen my mother in nearly forty years. After that, I might go around and see some old friends.'

'How long have you lived in Britain?'

'About eleven years.'

'You mean one-one?'

'Yes.'

'What do you do there?'

'I'm a journalist.'

'Do you have any documents that prove this?'

I reach into my pocket and take out my National Union of Journalists card. She glances at it and hands it back to me. 'What newspaper do you work for?'

'*Akhbar al-Arab*.'

She smiles, and I start to explain, 'It's an—'

'International paper,' she interrupts.

'You know it?'

'Ha! I'm from the Middle East. I know a lot about the Arab press. Is the name in the passport your actual name?'

'Since I was born in Asdud in 1948, I've only had one name. And my name has had only one owner—me. Walid Ahmad Dahman.'

Then there is the sound of my passport being stamped, and the clicking of my entry card being printed up. *Tik-tik-tak-tik*. My fear dissolves almost completely.

'Here you go, Mr. Dahman. Have a nice trip.' She hands me the passport through the little slot, along with my entry card. I thank her and go off to look for my baggage.

5

As I emerge from Exit Two, a cool breeze wafts over me. My eyes take in a picture-perfect scene of palm trees scattered about the airport entrance. One of the squat palms is so perfect that I have to stop and stare as the air plays with its tresses. The sunlight glimmers through the fronds like a string of pearls across the forehead of a beautiful girl.

I chastise the sun for hiding so shyly behind the palm—did my return surprise her that much? *For thirty-eight years I've longed to see the sun with its wheat-coloured complexion again. Only in Palestine does the sun take on this hue. To me, only you are the sun.*

The sun kisses me and begins to apologize. The warmth of her rays washes off the weariness of travel. The sound of my name comes to me in a whisper, *Walid.* I turn around to look and see only my shadow reaching through the glass door, stretching out through the long arcades inside the airport. The sight of my shadow is stunning. It is the first time I've ever seen my shadow on this particular piece of soil. It almost looks as if I am wearing a kuffiyya on my head. As if I am wearing an old galabiyya whose collar flaps in the breeze. My shadow clings to me, watching, like me, for the man who will take the both of us to the Beit Hanoun crossing. I am happy to know that for the rest of my trip, I will be accompanied by a shadow I have not seen for a long time.

I look all over, hoping to find the Palestinian-Israeli driver with whom I made arrangements to be picked up at 7 am. I look around, trying to find his car. 'It's a white VW van with green curtains,' he told me over the phone. I do not see the van, nor any man who is 'swarthy, medium build, wearing prescription eyeglasses', as he described himself to me two days ago. I imagined him as a doctor.

It is almost 8 am, which means that I am about an hour late for my pickup time. That is because the plane was delayed taking off, and then all that waiting in line at passport control. The man must have given up and gone home. I would not blame him if he did. I think about it for a while, then put it aside—this driver would come and he would wait and wait and wait as if he had nothing else to live for. If this was simply about helping a fellow countryman returning home for the first time in decades, he might not try so hard. But he would not give up on the hefty fare he was about to earn.

Shouts begin to rain down on me. Drivers hurl out the names of cities and towns—some of which stand on the carcasses of older cities and towns, others merely Hebraized. Yerushalim. Tel Aviv. Natanya. Nitsrit. Akko. Haifa. Herzliya.

Suddenly, I spot Dana walking toward a car parked close by. I watch her with mixed feelings. The woman who sat next to me on my journey will, in a matter of moments, disappear from my life for ever. A driver approaches her, dragging behind him the large suitcase that was beside her. He puts it into the trunk. She throws her handbag into the rear seat and then slides her body in as well. After that, she swings her legs in and closes the door. The car speeds off.

The drivers continue to sing out the names of cities to me. I reject them all, saying, *'Todah, todah!'* I am looking everywhere for Abu Fares.

I turn and spot a white van trying to park at the curb only a few cars away from me. I hurry toward it, pulling my bag behind me, and am happy to see the green curtains draped along the side windows. I pull out the paper on which I had written the licence plate number of Abu Fares' van. I guessed right—this is my car.

A man suddenly appears from behind it and strides toward me with confidence. He opens his arms wide to greet a long-exiled compatriot, 'Welcome, welcome home! So glad you made it safe and sound! I am so sorry—I've been driving around and around looking for a parking space. Welcome, fellow countryman! So glad to see you!' His two hands grasp my hand and shake it with genuine affection. I congratulate myself for my patriotic decision to choose a real local boy. *A Palestinian through and through.*

My lungs expand and drink in the scent of the place. Palestine. My eyes are filled with the visage of this man, the first man I meet who, unlike most of us Palestinians, did not leave in 1948.

'Thank you for such a warm welcome.'

'Give me your bags, you must be exhausted from your flight.'

Abu Fares takes my big suitcase and together we put it in the trunk. And then the car begins to move. This is my first journey inside the country I left as an infant.

Samir Ayash, one of the Palestinians I work with, told me: *'You're trip is going to be … very exciting.'* He said the last bit in English so I wouldn't miss it. *'You're going to drive past road signs that point back at all those old wounds, Ramleh, Jerusalem Road, Asqalan. You're going to see Asdud, aren't you?'*

I take out my mobile phone to call my mother and let her know I've arrived safely. *I cannot wait to get there, and I cannot believe I am actually here, in Palestine.* Abu Fares suddenly explodes: 'No, no, no, man! What do you think you're doing?' He yells so loudly that I am left wondering what I had done that was so wrong. *Maybe mobile use is prohibited here for security purposes?* With his left hand still on the steering wheel, Abu Fares' right hand shoots out and grabs the phone from my hand. 'Like hell you're going to use your phone here!'

Without taking his hand away from mine, he goes on. 'It's going to cost you a fortune to use your phone here. No, no, man! Give me the number and I'll dial it for you with mine. It's local. You're our guest, man! Understood?'

Abu Fares dials my mother's number on his phone, then hands it to me.

'Hi, Mama! I'm here. I'm home, Mama. I'm in Palestine!'

Uncontrollably, I begin to repeat these words into the phone. 'I'm here, Mama! I'm back home! I'm in Palestine!' Real tears stream down my cheeks. I listen to my mother's voice—only now does she begin to believe me. 'Yes, my son. You are home. Welcome, welcome! I can't wait to see you. Your cousins are going down to Beit Hanoun to wait for you.'

'No, no, Mama! Tell them not to go there until 9. I won't get to the crossing until after 9, maybe even a little later.'

I give the phone back to Abu Fares, who immediately asks, 'How long has it been, Abu … Abu …?'

'Abu Fadi. Almost forty years.'

'My God,' Abu Fares snorts. 'That's an entire lifetime. God help your mother—she's jumping for joy right about now, huh?'

Abu Fares' phone rings and he gives it to me. 'It's for you.'

'Hello? Welcome, cousin! Did you make it safely? Where are you?'

This must be Abdelfettah, my cousin on my mother's side. He must have got the number from my mother's phone.

'Hi, cousin! I'm on my way. We're driving right now.'

'We'll be at the crossing at the time we agreed. Where are you now?'

Abu Fares points toward the distance. 'That's Ramleh up ahead.'

Ramleh edges toward us, a white line drawn across a green billboard.

'We're at Ramleh, cousin. Don't go to Erez before 9.'

The car slows down, then stops at a traffic light.

I begin to look at the traffic sign, and study the name like someone who is spelling out the letters for the first time, R-a-m-l-eh. The arrow beneath points to the right. Underneath that, I read out 'Hayim Nahman Bialek Street.'

I laugh bitterly to myself—I am neither cool nor calm. *So Bialek gets to have a street named after him in Ramleh, but George Habash doesn't? Habash doesn't get a street named after him here, nor next door in Lod, where he was born, nor in Wahdat Camp in Amman, nor in the Republic of Fakahani in Beirut. Bialek who came from overseas gets to be a native of Ramleh, while Habash, native son of Lod, has to be a refugee far, far away.*

The light changes and Abu Fares speeds off again. All my senses are on alert, picking up every possibility. Every little thing that might prevent my memory from reaching into its past. But there is Abu Fares working to keep the door to the past wide open, and in doing so, he keeps my eyes wide open too. Their desire to see all this dispels their drowsiness.

'Over there is Ramleh's mosque. Do you see it, Abu Fadi? Over there, on the right.'

I turn to look where he points, even as the car speeds on. Behind a distant rise of cypress trees, a minaret flashes by, fleeing from my eyes. The image goes by so quickly that my eyes cannot really make it out.

'Do you know when we lost Lod and Ramleh, Abu Fadi?'

'Are you asking me, Abu Fares?' I am surprised that someone would even ask. I begin to recount the facts for him—how they were attacked by the Haganah in 1948, how they fell. He sits there listening to me as if it was the first time he had ever heard the story. When I finish, he comments, as if to soften the blow of all these memories: 'Lod was lost, and Ramleh was lost and so was the mosque. Some died and some were killed. Some went somewhere else and others emigrated and never came back. Some weren't able to take anything with them at all when they went. But you know, some Palestinians managed to stay put in Ramleh. They held on to what they had, then Palestinian refugees from elsewhere moved there too.'

'I've got a cousin from Ramleh,' I comment. 'Ismael Dahman is his name. He's got a daughter named Aisha in London and she goes home to visit once a year. She told me that Ramleh is not what it used to be. She says now it's mainly Ethiopians there. And collaborators. She says that since Oslo, Israel has used the city to resettle collaborators from Gaza.'

The car approaches another traffic signal where there is another green billboard. The olive-green colour of these signs is deceptive—it makes them seem like advertisements of peace. I begin to read the Hebrew while translating. Rishon LeZion. The First of Zion. Then Rehovot and Kfar Bilu.

The car stops at a third traffic light. While we wait, a young woman crosses the road. She is wearing a small black-and-red striped backpack. This is the first female Israeli soldier my eyes have seen since the 1956 occupation of Gaza. Suddenly I remember what my aunts said when they first laid eyes on female Israeli soldiers. These women wore trousers and took part in the foot patrols around the camps. 'Israeli women are like men,' they whispered to me. 'They even pee standing up.'

The car goes on its way and the names of cities begin to race after each other on the green traffic signs. Gan Shlomo-Kvutzat Schiller. Givat Brinner. Each one erases a signpost in my mind, and presents new facts for me to see.

Ashkelon 25 km. Was there really a place where it all began? Was there a beginning? For fifty-seven years, we have been counting our losses, sinking further and further into the distance. 1956: the War of Tripartite Aggression, the massacre of Khan Yunis. 1967: the Setback, and the loss of the remaining sliver of Palestine. 1973: the 6 of October War, in which Sadat triumphed over himself. 1982: the invasion of Lebanon and the expulsion of the PLO. Losses and endings giving birth to even more losses and endings. Then the Oslo

Accords. The beginning of another string of losses and endings—and not one of them the beginning of the real path back to Asqalan. Asqalan is right here now—only twenty-five kilometres away.

'You're thinking about something, aren't you! Should I take you back to Asdud? What do you say, Abu Fadi? We take a quick tour of Majdal, then head up to Asdud? The weather's gorgeous this morning—it makes you want to take a little detour, doesn't it?'

Unable to reply, I sigh. As I breathe in the distant past, my lungs begin to ache.

'Listen, it's only going to take two hours. I'll take you to Asdud and give you a quick tour, then we come right back. You want to see your hometown, don't you?'

'I wish it was on our way. We'd go there and I'd even pay good money for us to look at history together. But Asdud is too far away, Abu Fares. And my mother's waiting for me. She's been waiting for thirty-eight years for me to come home, and she doesn't have that much longer to live. I better go to see her first. Asdud can wait, my mother cannot. She's waiting to have breakfast with me, and I don't want to be late. She can't wait to see me.'

'OK, whatever's easiest.'

The car passes the exit for Asqalan and speeds through the barriers of my longing. Sderot begins to appear. From far off, it looks like a Swiss village, its red-tile roof houses carefully arranged behind thick green copses. Behind rows of trees, many of the houses look out over the main highway.

As soon as we cross into the city limits, the mirage begins to shed its splendour. The houses begin to fade, and the trees shed their leaves, as if getting ready to die. The soil loses all traces of verdure, and the grass turns barren and brown. Every distinctive feature of the place suddenly vanishes.

Abu Fares' car continues speeding down the highway, kicking up lifeless dirt and dust. This is how you know you are approaching Palestinian territory.

'We're here, Abu Fadi. That's the Beit Hanoun crossing over there.'

'Where?' I gasp.

'Up there, just ahead.'

Abu Fares parks the car and gets out. I get out too. Together, we pull the suitcase from the trunk.

I pull out my wallet, 'How much is it, Abu Fares? Name your price.'

'For you, I'm only charging one hundred and twenty dollars.'

I give Abu Fares the amount he asks for. He insists on hugging me. He gets into his car and races off towards Israel.

Suddenly, I am struck by the realization that Abu Fares charged me at least double the real fare. Bitterly, I shake my head. *Abu Fares is not a bad guy. He's a decent guy, no doubt. But he did trick me. He loves money more than his fellow countrymen. Foreign currency in particular, the distinctive smell of green dollars most of all.*

6

I get to the main entrance at about 9. The sky is clean and bright, washed by the early morning light. The sun hides behind a half-finished building, casting half-finished shadows across a quiet, dusty plaza littered with concrete blocks, rocks and gravel.

I stand there, staring at the inert scene before me. I am nervous and doubtful—and begin to wonder if Abu Fares took my one hundred and twenty dollars and dropped me off in the middle of nowhere. I take a few steps forward, pulling my suitcase behind me. Faint whispers sound in my ear and I wheel around, trying to find where the voices are coming from. My eyes spot three boys smoking cigarettes nearby. They are sitting on a long marble bench under a makeshift sunshade of asbestos pieces. Behind them, concrete encloses the awning from one side. The wall stretches off toward the west where it finally disappears into a small grove.

I walk up to the boys and say hello. I ask where I should go to cross. Two of them are only concerned with blowing clouds of smoke into the air. They go on talking to each other as if I was not there. The other one turns to me and nods: 'Over there, man.'

He points to a square kiosk that sits between two car lanes. Double wooden guard gates block each lane. My eyes follow his finger and I now see two Israeli soldiers walking in front of the gates, American-made M-16 rifles strapped across their backs. There is a rectangular opening on the façade of the kiosk, like a small window. The torso of a young female soldier fills most of it. *I will go over there right now. I will present myself to the upper half of the Israeli soldier, or to one of the other soldiers.*

I grab my suitcase and start walking toward them. One of the boys shouts at me, 'Where you going, man? The crossing is closed!'

He is obviously right. I probably got here too early. I guess I will wait until it opens. I will have to trust these guys—they obviously know. 'When does it open?'

'God only knows!' One of them shrugs, as if the opening and closing of the crossing was a fact of life he was used to. Then he points at the two soldiers, whose marching brings them to a halt in front of the guard gates. They exchange a few words, then turn and head off in opposite directions. As the boy's friends kick at the gravel under the bench, he adds: 'Those are the ones who know.' He points at them again.

I stand there like a piece of wood, unable to ask any more questions. One of the other boys finally notices me and calls out in a tired voice: 'Listen, man. We got here a little while ago, and it was already closed. Why it's closed is anybody's guess.'

'He's not from here,' the other one says, looking me over. He studies me like I was an artifact, then asks bluntly, 'Where're you from?'

'London.'

'If you've got a British passport, you won't have any problems. Foreigners have it easy. You can go through the VIP entrance as soon as they open.'

The way he pronounces 'VIP' makes it sound like a magic word. I am relieved to hear that I will be getting the kind of special treatment reserved for only the Very Important. When the crossing opens, I will not have to walk over to the soldiers to explain myself. I will not have to beg from the torso of the woman in the kiosk. Only now does it begin to dawn on me how important I truly am. I have an official stamp that attests to my special status, and it will command respect. I rank among the top of the topmost—foreigners who enjoy the privileges granted by the Oslo Accords only to PA ministers and employees of foreign NGOs. We have an importance that no ordinary Palestinian could ever hope to attain—and according to the terms of the Accords, ordinary Palestinians are simply ordinary, which is to say, neither important nor very important. I admit that it is embarrassing to be considered so important, but I am also pleased—and the pleasure is audible in my voice. 'So that means I'll get in, right?'

'If they open the crossing,' says the first boy, as if he was the official spokesman for the group. This 'if' hangs in the air—the only tangible fact waiting for me in the plaza. I notice that already the half-finished shadows have begun to inch their way back to the foot of the half-finished structure.

'When will they open it?'

'Anyone's guess.' Another one of them lets out a sarcastic laugh and crosses his legs like we are all sitting around at a pavement café. 'Listen, man—those Jews over there, they'll open their crossing whenever they want to. And they'll close it again whenever they want.'

The only thing for me to do is to study the place until I figure out how it works. One of the things I had not taken into account in planning my trip was that I would arrive to find the crossing was shut. Today is not a Jewish holiday, which means the crossing is not closed, on the pretext of preventing a Palestinian attack. And the Egyptian-sponsored truce between Israel and the factions had held steady since March. There have been no suicide attacks or bombings, even though Israel continued its assassination campaign against Palestinian leaders and activists. In fact, I had taken all these things into account and would not have attempted to come to Gaza had I thought there might be fighting. And as much as my mother would like to see me, she did not want me delivered to her doorstep in a coffin.

Why did they close it? No answer. Everything had been going pretty well until now. Things were not as bad as I had imagined they would be—not on the plane, not at the airport. My luck was too good to hold for ever.

In a daze, I stand near the three boys, too paralysed to do anything. For these guys, this was a routine part of a normal day—but it is hard for me to be nonchalant about it. *Should I leave? Should I go back the way I came? Where would I go if I did? Should I stay here, waiting? How long?* As my questions expand, my estimated time of arrival begins to change too—everything about my trip seems to need rethinking. My trip did not begin the moment I boarded the plane at Heathrow. It did not begin when I met the Israeli actress. It did not begin with those farfetched stories she told me to break the ice. No, my journey home begins right now—in this half-abandoned plaza, standing before these gates.

I study the crossing and everything in it. A vast building situated between two worlds. They sit there, these gates of hell, on a long rise about fifty metres from where I am. In front of it stand three massive concrete pedestrian barriers. To the left, a squat single-storey structure. Male and female soldiers come in and out, their weapons clanking loudly enough to tell the world how ready they are to be used. To the right, there is a thicket of cypress and willow. Their leafy branches completely screen the western side of the building.

On the other side of this gate live one-and-a-half million Palestinians. The people who live there—and the settlements around them—form another world, whose doors shut tight on this spot. Here is the syphon where, early each morning, long lines of Gazan workers drain into Israel, and where, when night falls, they are flushed back out, exhausted by their twelve- or fifteen-hour shifts. Youths born between the two Intifadas burn up their lives travelling this short span. Filling the construction industry, factories, building the walls of Jewish settlements. They probably even built this huge processing plant itself that churns and crushes the people twice a day, first as they exit Gaza and then again as they re-enter.

I put my suitcase down to the side, then sit on a shaded piece of concrete near to where the three boys still sit—chatting, laughing, and smoking up a storm.

A little after 9 am groups of people start to get dropped off in front of the main gate. There are men and women of all ages, and children too. They begin to take their places here and there around the plaza as if they were permanent refugees. They fill the place with the same question I had been asking—and over and over again, they receive the same old answer: 'God only knows.'

A large bus enters the plaza and parks not too far away. The driver points the front of the bus toward the crossing so he can watch for things happening there. He backs up the bus until it is almost pissing against the cement wall.

The driver does not get out. He does not start asking people the same old question, and he does not wait to hear that the only one who knows anything here is God. Most likely, he has already heard it all before.

Within an hour, the shaded areas fill up with crowds of people and the plaza has turned into a vast open-air waiting room. Under the beating sun, the soldiers shout louder and louder at the crowds to remind them that they alone hold the keys to the gate.

A sky-blue Opel enters the plaza and parks near the bus. When the rock under my butt gets tired of complaining, I give it a rest. I start walking back and forth, dragging my suitcase behind me from one spot to another. I listen in to the conversations between the newcomers and the others around the plaza. Some of them find a place to sit under the sunshade. Others make a spot for themselves on the ground in the shade of the long wall just behind it. Others sit in the shadow of the Opel. Three women get out of the bus and sit in its shade while their children play under the sun.

A young man in overalls comes up. Another man runs over to him and they exchange some words before the first man disappears again. The second one comes back and begins to make an announcement to everyone: 'That man works here—and he told me that the soldiers found a bomb in a paper bag.'

A chunky man in his thirties walks up and asks, 'What are you saying? Really?'

'God only knows—but that's what that guy I was talking to just told me.'

My whole trip, exploded by a briefcase. If it's true, they're not going to open up the gate for me or anyone else today.

From behind the Opel, a voice calls out: 'Don't believe it, folks. There was nothing but tomatoes in the briefcase. Four big tomatoes. One of the workers accidentally left it at the main gate.' No one can see who says this.

A woman in a hijab yells out, 'Fuck them! They shut down the entire border crossing on account of four goddamn tomatoes?'

'They made one of the Palestinians who works there pick up the case and empty it out. And then they made the poor guy take apart each tomato, picking out the seeds one by one! I can't help thinking that those tomato bombs would have been perfect with okra.'

I laugh at the kitchen explosive, and at the rumours that fly around faster than facts could ever do. I laugh at everyone standing around. One of them blurts out: 'Since the bomb was just some tomatoes, they'll have to open up and let us through now.'

'If only every bomb were a tomato—and not the precious blood of our children,' comments an old woman. She sounds like she has lost someone. A small waking dream begins to stir in my mind—small, no bigger than a tomato seed.

But the crossing remains as closed as it was before, even as the crowds of arrivals grow and grow, and the flow of conversation returns to its usual channels.

Behind the guard gates and the kiosk, a small truck enters the plaza and comes to a stop in front of the concrete barriers by the main building. Soldiers run into the plaza behind the guard booth, in a way that makes everyone nervous. A military jeep surges from behind the thicket of trees and parks close to the barriers. Two soldiers jump out and disappear behind the truck. Two men and a woman in uniform walk into the plaza. One of them is carrying a video camera on his shoulder. A young man who had been sitting by the wall stands up and walks over to me. A transistor radio dangles from his hand. In a trembling voice he says: 'Israeli radio just reported that they caught a girl from Jabalia Camp wearing an explosives belt.'

All my hopes of them opening the crossing go up in smoke. The news tears my dreams to shreds, and I start to envy Adel El-Bashity for how easy he had it. No matter the lengths to which a narrator goes in order to imagine something, he will never reach the shore of truth. If your understanding of an Israeli border crossing is limited to what you hear or try to imagine in your mind, you will only ever glimpse the outlines of a shadow—which could be shorter or longer depending on how much light you cast on it. But the truth itself: that is a bitch on the imagination and on anyone who wants to tell a story.

It is now 11:30. The June sun has begun to shed its morning gentleness to announce the pending arrival of a scorching afternoon. The shady spots have disappeared. There is not even enough shade now for a quarter of the people standing there.

I begin to look for a shady spot, one for myself and one for my shadow, which has shrunk so small that were I to lend it out, it would not cover a soul. I head toward the bus and shyly lean up against it, by the front door. Just as the years of my youth now lean upon my old age, I rest my head on the side of the door.

The driver sits calmly behind the steering wheel, like a feudal lord who owns vast orchards of shade. He is engrossed in conversation with a young man sitting in a seat directly behind him.

The driver suddenly turns to me and, with a note of pity in his voice, says, 'Why are you standing outside, sir? Come on in and have a seat. The sun out there will roast your brains. It looks like you've already come a long way just to get to here.'

I do not hesitate to accept his invitation. In fact, since resting my head against the door, I had been hoping he might say that. This is my chance to take a break from the strain of standing and pacing back and forth all morning. I might even join their conversation and kill some time—and maybe kill this wait that has been killing my every hope of crossing sometime soon.

I climb into the bus and take my place in the first seat to the right of the driver, just behind the door itself. To break the ice, I ask: 'Where'd you all come from today?'

'Jerusalem.'

'The bus is empty—is that usual?'

'We're a company that provides services for the UN. We work by contract. We take people to visit family members in prison. On Friday I go to Gaza to pick up families who're going to visit people in Beersheba prison. But if the crossing doesn't open in a couple of hours, we won't be able to do it. What a waste of my time and theirs. And those poor people—they've been waiting so long for this trip. Now they'll have to go through the same rigmarole just to get another permit.'

The driver's mobile phone rings, he answers it with his left hand. His keeps his right on the steering wheel, ready to go at any moment. 'No, we're still at the checkpoint. I'm sitting here in the bus with these good folks. We're still waiting for them to open up so we can go through. They're saying there was an attempt. Tell him to go back to the West Bank. Tell Abu Khalil to go to Qalqilia and bring everyone. No, no—if they don't open up in one hour, two maximum, I'm going back. What else can I do? Goodbye. No, don't worry—I'll bring them with me from Jerusalem. *Salaam*.'

He hangs up. A short, dark-skinned young man walks up to the door. He sticks his head in and comments nervously: 'If there really was a bombing attempt like they say, then the crossing is going to stay shut all day long. It might not even re-open until after tomorrow.'

'What a disaster,' I mutter. 'Where should I go?'

The younger man turns to me. 'Where are you coming from, sir?'

'London.'

'England?'

'Yes.' Despite myself, I begin to wonder aloud. 'Where should I go? I can't get through and I can't go back into Israel. If I go to Israel, where would I spend the night? I didn't anticipate this at all.'

'No problem!' The man interrupts me. 'As long as we're here, you can stay in the West Bank. You're our guest! What do you say? Come with us and we'll take good care of you, sir!'

I decide to jump at his offer before he rescinds it. 'If the crossing doesn't re-open, where will you go?'

'We're going back to Hebron, and you'll come with us. I've got a car. That blue Opel over there.' He points to the car, then to a woman who is walking up to him right at that moment. Then to a boy and girl who begin to chase each other. He introduces them to me, 'This is my family. My wife. These kids you see jumping around—they're mine.'

When the man's wife smiles at me, she opens up a familiar window into my heart and fills it with hope and warmth. 'We're all in it together. Consider me your sister. You'll come with us.'

Before I have a chance to respond, her husband adds: 'Don't worry about it. Our home is your home.'

'Bless you, you're kind. And come to think of it, I have an uncle and some cousins in Hebron.'

'What's their name?'

'The Dahmans. From Asdud. My uncle is Jamil Abdelfettah...'

'You mean Abu Salah? My God!'

'Yes, exactly—that's him. Abu Salah is my mother's brother. Do you know him?'

'Of course we do—he's our neighbour. He lives two doors down from us. I know his children—Salah, Khidr and Shaher—all of them. Can you believe it? Turns out we're neighbours! But with all respect to your uncle and cousins, you're spending your first night in Hebron with us!'

I breathe a sigh of relief when I hear this. But my temporary Hebron idyll is cut short by the voice of the bus driver who announces that he does not want to wait any longer. 'Sorry, folks, but it's time to pack up and go home.'

He turns the ignition and the man from Hebron steps off the bus. I get off too, followed by the young man who had been sitting right behind the driver the whole time.

The three women who had been sitting next to the bus stand up and relinquish the sliver of shade they had been using to cover their bodies. The bus pulls out of the plaza, leaving behind a cloud of dust and a empty, bright space. Everyone who had been sitting there goes elsewhere, looking for shade.

A voice calls out from the middle of the plaza: 'There she is, they're taking her to the *Mukhabarat!*'

At that, all eyes turn to look at the main building. There is a woman wearing a hijab and a thin black galabiyya. Two soldiers are escorting her, and she is carrying something I cannot quite make out. They walk out of the building, then disappear behind the military vehicle.

I cannot believe that I am watching a failed suicide attack, that I am seeing it unfold with my own eyes.

I cannot believe that I am watching a woman who was about to detonate a bomb on her body, and with that, blow the remnants of the current cease-fire to smithereens. And, I might add, explode my dream of getting into Gaza.

Suddenly, this whole scene seems fascinating to me as a writer. I start to forget how hot it is. I forget how tiring it is. How long I have been waiting, and how tedious it is. It begins to dawn on me that I am actually fortunate; I have jumped into a scene that Adel El-Bashity never experienced.

This is a rare occurrence, I tell myself, trying to wrest some bit of good luck from what is, in strategic terms, a setback. I want to take some photos. I stick my hand inside my backpack and feel for the video camera. Then I stop myself. My hand comes out empty as soon as I remember that doing something like this is sure to cause me all sorts of trouble, and some people will not find it amusing if I begin to take pictures. First, I did not get a permit from the Israeli press office in Jerusalem. Second, they could begin to fire at me, or drag me over, break my camera and detain me. They might then deport me. This is the sort of situation where one does not take risks. I repress my journalistic instinct to record. I will write it all down instead. I think about writing up a report, relating the events I have experienced since this morning. The bag of tomatoes. That is not possible. What if the soldiers in the guard booth take notice of me? What if there are others who are watching us from further off? Do not sit down and start writing here. That would be foolish, the prelude to a bad ending.

A sense of despair creeps over me. My journalistic self falls prey to hesitation and fear.

7

The only thing about the girl that blows up is her attempt. She walks back to where she came from, trailing her black galabiyya behind her. The same two soldiers escort her. Two other soldiers leap out from behind the military truck and run toward the jeep parked in front of the building, about thirty metres from where I am standing. They get into the jeep and take their places in front of computer screens.

A young man next to me is staring at the scene, and I ask him what is going on. He explains that the jeep is the mobile headquarters for remote control operations. The soldiers operate robots via their computers.

Cameras in hand, three television journalists suddenly emerge from the thicket of trees, then disappear behind the building. No sooner do they disappear from our sight than an Israeli soldier comes to escort them toward the guard booth where they stand as if awaiting orders.

A boy yells out, 'Mama, I have to pee!'

I look over to where the voice is coming from and I see a woman holding the hand of a boy who cannot be older than four. He is jumping up and down while clenching his other hand between his thighs as if his bladder was about to explode. *This is a place that really deserves to be pissed on.* The two of them walk over to a doorless cement block.

From behind the truck, a small robot bursts into view. It looks like a metal spider, with a long skinny arm that sticks out about half a metre into the air, from which dangles a strap. Slowly, the robot rolls forward toward the right of the building. It disappears behind the jeep then pops out again for a few seconds before going into the trees. And then I cannot see it any more. I doubt if anyone else can.

I remember the first time I ever saw footage of a robot. One of the Arab satellite channels was rebroadcasting film from Israeli television. The robot was dragging the corpse of a Palestinian man who had blown himself up. As the robot pulled the body, it painted a thick stripe of blood, which traced down the street all the way until it reached the jeep where the pieces of the body were collected.

The three-person television crew is still there with its military escort. They take a few steps from the spot next to the guard booth where they had been made to stand. Then they all—television crew and escort—sprint toward the main building and disappear somewhere behind.

The woman and child return. After draining his bladder in the outdoor urinal, the boy looks relieved, even happy. He hops and skips all the way back to where they had been standing before.

At exactly 1 pm an explosion shakes the entire area,

and my body shudders to feel it. Dense smoke rises from behind the thicket of trees, and with it all traces of the attempt.

The camera crew go back to their spot. An officer comes up to them and stands in front of one of their cameras. He begins to deliver a statement that none of us in the plaza can hear. A spokesman from the Israeli army, no doubt briefing the media on what transpired here this morning.

The camera crew wraps things up and quickly leaves the plaza. They walk right through all of us and disappear. At this point, everyone begins to murmur: 'Now they're going to open up the crossing.'

8

I find myself staring at a man sitting in a wheelchair. He is wearing a baseball cap that hides half his face and his hands lie wilted on the armrests. His body is so slight, anyone could lift him and his chair at the same time.

The man swelters in the afternoon sun and is trying his best to gather his body beneath the shade of his hat. After some hesitation, I walk over to him. 'The sun is too much, sir. Can I walk you over to the shade?' I point toward a patch of unused shadow extending out from under the sunshade.

The man does not answer. He does not even raise his eyes to look at me. He shows no signs of wanting to see the face of a stranger who has offered to help him. He merely waves me away with his hand. *Forget about it.*

Is it pride or embarrassment? Or pure recklessness? I think for a moment and decide not to give up. 'I'm only trying to help.'

'I'm used to it, man. It's not my first time sitting here and it won't be the last. Whenever I go to Ramallah for treatment and try to come back, it's always the same old crap.'

The loudspeaker interrupts us. I cannot make out

what the voice is saying, but it ends my attempt to convince the man to let me help him.

As soon as the announcement is repeated, everybody begins to sprint toward the guard booth. Only then do I understand what the announcement was: that people should bring their identity cards and entry permits to the checkpoint kiosk.

The man in the wheelchair lifts his head toward me slightly, as if taking his leave. He smiles as he begins to roll toward the crossing.

Nearly all the men have disappeared from the plaza. Only women remain. After handing their IDs and permits to their male relatives, they stay with the infants and young children.

A handsome young man in glasses comes over to the man in the wheelchair and takes his identity card. The older man does not stop him as he walks over to the checkpoint kiosk. The man passes the identity card to a tall soldier with a face as red as a ripe tomato. The soldier stacks the cards and permits on top of one another in a large pile.

The young man returns to stand next to me. I am still standing exactly where I was. I have not moved at all, as if what is going on around me has nothing to do with me, or as if I had not been waiting for this moment for hours. I am genuinely confused about what is expected of me. The man in the wheelchair explains that what I am supposed to do is present my papers to the soldier at the kiosk. But as I understand it, the kiosk has nothing to do with me, since VIPs, I thought, were supposed to present them at the VIP entrance, which is on the other side of the checkpoint.

I hesitate before asking the young man next to me: 'Excuse me, but where do people with passports go?'

Rather than answer me, he asks, 'What kind of passport?'

'British.'

He tells me give it to the soldier at the checkpoint kiosk. Then he mentions the fact that he himself carries a UN passport, and that he handed it in along with everyone else when they presented their identity cards and permits.

I pull my suitcase behind me as I walk over to the kiosk. I hand my passport to the soldier, who takes it without looking at me. He puts it in the pile with all the other papers. Then he shouts in Arabic: 'Anyone else with an ID or permit?'

Another young man walks up to him and hands him two cards. The soldier disappears inside the kiosk while everyone stands around waiting.

The young man with the UN passport joins the crowd outside the kiosk. 'Now what happens?' I ask.

'They inspect them in batches, then they call out people's names. When you hear your name, you can go through.'

'And the passports?'

'They take them to the office over there.' He points to the VIP office. Hearing this helps me calm down—it means that I am still very important, even if my passport is temporarily sitting alongside the other, less important travel papers in the soldier's hand.

I go on waiting like everybody else—under the burning sun and with no shred of shade in which to take refuge except for the small one cast by my own body. Close by, I notice a five-year-old boy entertaining himself by kicking the ground with his foot. On his head, he wears a hat that he must have made out of green upholstery. Next to him stands a girl a couple of years older. She holds up her hands to shield her eyes from the glare of the sun. And a baby resting on her mother, sucking away at a pacifier, trying to find shade under the kerchief her mother holds over their heads. An old woman wraps her head in white gauze as she sits on the ground. Then I notice her bare feet. I am startled and begin to watch her. She mumbles to herself then lifts herself off the sun-baked gravel. She goes looking for shade under the utility pole.

I walk over to the pole and lean up against it, doubling the size of the slice of shade the old woman now sits in.

When I walk away again, my shadow splits from the pole's and leaves the woman in full sunlight. As I go by, she looks up, shading her eyes with a hand into which time has etched the lines of her life. The other hand blocks out the light of the sun, and she studies me with a quick glance.

I bend down on my knees. 'Good afternoon, ma'am.'

'And to you, son.'

The way she pronounces 'son'—with a wide open 'o' sound—makes my heart open wide in turn, like the sails of a small boat when a sweet breeze hits them. 'Have you been sitting in this scorching heat for a long time, ma'am?'

'More than two hours, son. What am I supposed to do? Yesterday, I had a bypass operation in Ramallah, and today I'm trying to get home. I've been going through checkpoint after checkpoint all day since early this morning. Sometimes the traffic moves, most times it doesn't. And here I am, sitting and waiting until God frees us from this misery.'

'Where are you headed to, ma'am?'

'I'm trying to get back to Absan. Do you know where Absan is, son? You don't look like you're from around here.'

'Do I know where Absan is? Of course I do—I know both Absans. I also know Khazaa!'

'You speak like us, but you've got an accent from God knows where. You're not from Absan are you?'

I sit down next to her. 'When I was young, ma'am— when I was seventeen, I worked as a foreman for a contractor by the name of Abu Nabih Hejazi. We built the water tower in Absan and the one in Khazaa too.'

'You haven't been back in a while, have you?'

'Not in thirty-eight years.'

'Your poor mother. If I were her, I would have torn my hair out in grief. Is she still alive, son?'

'Thankfully, yes. She's been waiting for me to arrive since early this morning.'

'God save us from this scorching sun. I wish God would throw them all into hell!'

This poor woman—what can I do? Stand over her and give her shade? Give her my suitcase to sit on?

Damn my awkwardness—it is only there to remind me how powerless we are. Suddenly, I get an idea. I open my backpack and take out a pair of Reeboks. I put them down next to the woman's feet.

'What's this, son?'

'Put them on your feet, ma'am. It is like walking on hot coals out here.'

'I'm used to it, my boy. These look expensive.'

I lean over and help put them on. She tries to bat away my hands as she mumbles, 'Please don't. Really!' Her embarrassment is as advanced as she is.

I pay no attention to her protests. 'Don't be so shy, consider me like your son, ma'am.' I finish tying her shoes then stand up and go back to the pole. The old woman sits there throughout, calling out prayers in a voice so loud it fills the plaza. I lean up against the pole, lending the old woman some shade. I stand there as the minutes go by and the sadness of the scene finally gets to me. As tears begin to roll down my cheeks, I wipe them away. I wipe away my sadness too.

A skinny, tall soldier begins to shout at the crowd in an agitated voice: 'Everybody needs to step back!' And he begins to push people away from the guard booth.

A young man comes out of the crowd and begins to yell back at him. He does not bother to conceal his frustration. 'You want me to leave this elderly man standing in the sun? That's not right.' He points to an old man bent over a cane. The cane trembles in the old man's hands, as if he were just learning how to use it. The old man begins to drag his feet away from the guard booth.

'Everybody has to step back, like everybody else. Young and old, no exceptions. Go on, get back!' The soldier goes on yelling as if we were deaf.

Finally, everyone steps back. An officer standing there grabs a small wooden chair at the wall and gives it to the old man. He then turns to the soldier and tells him not to worry about the old man. The soldier gathers up his spite and begins to hurl it doubly hard at everyone else. 'Get the hell away from here! Get the hell back!'

The same young man walks up to the old man and helps him sit down in the chair in the shade by the wall. The old man puts his cane between his knees and rests his chin on it. I begin to study him more closely. The wrinkles on his face look like they were drawn by an artist wanting to depict a difficult and tired life. An entire life leaning on a cane at a border crossing. He reminds me of Ismail Shammout's iconic painting, *We Will Return*. I imagine him walking straight into the picture and taking the place of the old man there. Did Shammout know that the Nakba would reproduce, generation after generation—and that with each new Nakba we would look again at his painting and reconsider the words, *We Will Return*? Did he know that we would read those words over and over again throughout the years, even though we never did return?

'Everybody back, I said!' The soldier starts up again—as if he was a screaming machine. 'We're not collecting IDs right now. Get in line. We'll do it one by one. You know the rules.'

You son of a bitch—if there were any real rules, we would not be sitting here all day in the hot sun waiting to walk one hundred metres across a piece of land that belongs to us in the first place.

The crowd begins to rush toward the kiosk, ignoring the man's shouts. Sheepishly, I go along with everyone else. I am not at all accustomed to this kind of chaos—how it drives you on and changes how you act. It turns us into mayhem professionals who hate rules because we do not know what they look like.

The soldier begins collecting another batch of identity cards and permits from people who have just arrived. Then he stops abruptly, leaving dozens of hands hanging in mid-air, and dozens of voices pleading and wishing him all sorts of good things. 'God bless you, sir!' This man, for whom you wish nothing but a quick death, is suddenly the beneficiary of multiple prayers for a long, happy life. But this loud outpouring of well-wishing saves no one from his cruelty. He disappears, taking with him the new IDs and permits.

A couple of soldiers come forward and begin to push people away with their hands. I stand there, too timid to do anything, as if the soldier's words were what planted me in my place. Then the crowd, like a wave crashing on the beach, plucks me up and tosses me behind the guardrail.

The officer now turns to the old man and begins to shout. 'You've got to go too, old man. Come on, get up!'

'Shame on you! He's an elderly man. Don't you have a father?'

Now a young woman holding a child joins in: 'Don't you have family?'

For a moment, the officer ignores her, then he wheels round and shouts at her: 'You—you get back right now. Everybody back. No exceptions.'

The old man leans on his cane to stand up. He walks away with slow, heavy steps. He exits this little painting and returns to the real-life tableau of hundreds of Palestinians trying to get through the crossing. The old man steps aside, leans over and then sits down on the ground. The hot stones beneath him are like those in a bread oven.

From afar, I begin to study the officer. A stock character, straight out of central casting—the heroic guard standing at the gate, protecting the borders against the assaults of barbaric goyim. He comes back home at the end of each month and tells stories about how he could handle crowds of angry Palestinians all by himself. Bragging about how he deserves a promotion for so effectively abusing elderly Palestinian men. About how this checkpoint would break others who were not up to the task of working in the elite ranks of the Givati Brigade, the pride of the entire IDF.

I begin to shout at the soldier and the sound of my voice rips my insides apart and returns me to reality. In that very moment, I gather up my old self and push forward like everyone else around me—a refugee stranded at the threshold of his homeland.

'You there—get out! Get away!' The officer yells at me, and I find myself stripped down to nothing, nothing but the capacity to be yelled at and shooed away. I retreat with the crowd now trickling back toward the shade. I drag my suitcase and my disappointment behind me as I walk back. I cannot get the scene or the officer out of my mind.

By now I am tired. I have spent more than four hours in this detention centre. I look around for some shade— but most of the good spots are taken. I spy a wooden barrel in the shade and I rush over.

With a tissue, I wipe the sticky, crusty sweat from my forehead. I begin to stare at this officer, who has begun to build settlements in my mind.

9

Everyone is still standing around, waiting. Another half hour goes by, then a teenage soldier comes out of the kiosk. In her hand she is carrying a bunch of identity cards and permits. She begins to call out to the people they belong to. My eyes are glued to the pile of documents she is holding, trying to see whether my passport is among them.

The people whose names she calls gather around a wooden guardrail. The girl tells them to head over to the main building. She leaves and goes over to the VIP building.

Ten more minutes go by, then the girl comes back to the kiosk. She puts down her rifle and in a single breath rattles off a long list of names. She calls out the name of the old lady going to Absan. Off she goes, her feet slipping around in the Reeboks I gave her. My eyes cannot believe what they are seeing, my feet rejoice at the sight. For a few moments I forget all my waiting and impatience. Watching the woman helps to relax me. She seems to float across the scorched earth. *She reminds me of all the mothers who live on the other side of these gates.* As she disappears into the main building, I begin to cry again—the person she reminds me of is my own mother, still waiting somewhere over there.

The girl stops calling out the names on the new list, and for a second time, I do not hear mine among them. I look around and notice that the blue Opel has disappeared. They probably went into the main building when I was not looking. The invitation to stay with them in Hebron has now obviously expired.

Another soldier comes up to the group still standing around the desk. She has walked over from the VIP building carrying another stack of travel documents. Because there are so few in this bunch, I can see mine among them. She immediately begins to read off the names. I can feel the moment of my release drawing near. A few seconds from now, she is going to call my name. But when she gets to my passport she suddenly removes it and places it at the bottom of the stack again. She reads the name on the next document, and the man it belongs to rushes through the turnstile. Then the next one, and another man goes through as well.

I cannot stand it any longer and I shout in English, 'Please, isn't it my turn?'

'What kind of passport do you have?'

'British. It's the passport right there in your hands.'

She flips it open and glances at it. 'Are you Walid Dahman?'

I nod my head.

'Wait here,' she tells me as she tosses my passport onto a desk inside the kiosk. Then she whispers a few words in Hebrew to the soldier standing inside. He takes the passport and goes off toward the special office where the VIP documents are inspected.

By now, it is almost 2 pm. I never anticipated it would drag on this long. Hours ago, I was supposed to sit down with my mother for a breakfast of olives and zaatar. Suddenly, my British citizenship seems ridiculous. Whatever importance I possess because of it turns out to be not very important at all. I now regret coming here. The experience begins to erode my sense of being. What little humanity I have has been pulverized and scattered to the wind.

A young man who overhears the conversation comes up and tries to console me. 'Don't worry, sir. It's normal for them to take foreign passports over to the VIP building for inspection. Then they bring them back and call out your name right here. You'll get to cross—just be patient. You won't have to wait much longer.'

'If that was all it was, I wouldn't be complaining. But we've been putting up with this crap since first thing this morning.'

'This is nothing compared to what they do sometimes. I swear to you, at Qalqilia I've seen women giving birth.'

Shortly after, a man returns from the VIP building, carrying a number of documents. He hands them to the girl, who pulls out my passport from among them and calls out my name: 'Walid Dahman!'

I leap over to her. My feet never even touch the ground. I grab the passport. Only as I am starting to go through the turnstile do I remember to go back for my suitcase. I lug my baggage behind me, the soldier giggling at me the whole time.

When I walk into the VIP building, I set my suitcase down on the floor. This waiting room is sparsely furnished and dingy. A brown-skinned man, a janitor by his appearance, comes up to me and tells me in Palestinian: 'Your suitcase stays outside.'

It is easy to see these are probably 'security measures'—but are they really necessary for an office that does not allow suicidals or smugglers to enter in the first place? I pull my suitcase back outside and set it down next to the other suitcases there, then I come back inside.

I hand my passport to a tall, young soldier with a red face and pumpkin-orange hair. He is polite as he takes it. He asks me about my destination and the address where I will be staying in the Gaza Strip. I tell him all he needs to know. 'I'm going to visit my mother and cousins.'

To speed things up, I add a few details to give my story some drama and to make things seem even more natural—my seventy-six-year-old mother cannot walk and I have not seen her in thirty-eight years.

Without saying anything, he hands me a two-page application form and asks me to fill it out. I do, and sign it, and hand it back to him.

'What's your mother's name?'
'Amina Dahman.'

'What's her ID number and her address?'

'Um, I didn't know that information was required.'

'We need the ID number and address of someone in Gaza.'

'How am I supposed to know that? All I know is that my mother lives in Khan Yunis Camp.'

'We need an ID number.'

Once again, my hopes of entering Gaza begin to fade. I realize that my wait, which has already gone on for more than five hours, will now last a few more. I may well be stuck here with this soldier for an age. Or with the next soldier who takes his place on the late night shift.

My mobile rings and I get an idea. It is my cousin Abdelfettah who has been waiting with everybody else on the Palestinian side. I tell him what is going on and ask him to see what he can do to get my mother's ID number. Abdelfettah says he will call my mother's neighbour Majda who has a key. Majda will look for the ID and call us back with the number.

I relay all this to the soldier, telling him that it might take some time. I suggest that he might just look up my mother's number in the databanks. 'Please, sir. She's been waiting to see me since she woke up this morning.'

He appears to be sympathetic and asks for my mother's name. I tell him her name again. He tells me to wait until I hear my name called.

I go over and sit down on a black leather chair near the door. I stretch out my legs and sink into the backrest—into my first break since I arrived at the crossing so many hours ago. I look around. Three small waiting rooms linked by a corridor. Each room furnished with a row of leather chairs pushed together, directly across from the offices of the security personnel.

The fresh air dries the sweat of the day and begins to soothe the sunburn of waiting. The part of my soul that has been taken from me today begins to return, wafting back on the strains of the music that plays in the waiting rooms.

Less than ten minutes go by before the same soldier calls over to me to say that he has located my mother's ID number and address. I start to walk over to his desk, thinking that he is about to stamp an entry visa into my passport. But with a wave of his hand, he stops me in my tracks and motions for me to return to my seat. When he opens his mouth, he speaks the language of order and command: 'Don't move. Stay right where you are until I tell you to move. Understand?'

He tosses my passport to a co-worker sitting at the other end of the desk. The man turns it over and inspects the cover. He opens it up and leisurely flips through the pages before tossing it onto the desk as if it were nothing.

A Hebrew-language song suddenly comes over the loudspeaker. Nearby, a girl begins to sway back and forth to the rhythm. As her swaying turns into dance, the M16 slung across her back begins to swing back and forth like a pendulum. The girl disappears down a side corridor only to reappear from the other side. She walks right past me, looking down at me as she goes by. Then she goes out of the door.

New arrivals pour in all the time. They begin by presenting their documentation, then take their seats wherever they can. While this is going on, the people who were here before me begin to retrieve their documents, now with the visa stamp on them. No one hesitates. They depart for Gaza immediately.

An entire hour goes by. It is approaching 3 pm now and I have not heard my name called yet. Nor has anyone come to get me. I decide to test how very important my person is, and walk over to the soldier on whose desk my passport is sitting. 'I've been waiting here for over an hour now. Will it take much longer?'

He pretends not to know who I am. He even acts as if it was not he who, just an hour ago, was inspecting my passport as if it were a dangerous contagion. He lifts his head. 'What's your name?'

'Walid Ahmad Dahman.'

He takes a piece of paper from a file on his desk and hands it to me. 'Fill out this form and sign it, Mr. Walid.'

I take it and glance at it then object, 'But I already filled out a form like this and gave it to your colleague.'

'This copy is for me.'

Since I do not want to make things worse, I follow his orders like a conscript. I even flash him a salute. 'Yes, sir! Here you go—another form, all filled out for you. Complete with my signature and everything.'

'Sit back down. Don't come over here again unless someone calls out your name.'

I go back to my seat, but find that a large man has taken my place. He sits there flirting in Hebrew with a girl soldier who is standing next to him. The dark-skinned janitor reappears and winks at me. The man never stops moving as he cleans the place. I step back while he joins their jokey circle. The entire time, he continues to sweep the ground in front of my feet.

The boredom and weariness of the scene finally get to me. My chest tightens and I can feel the tension inside. It intensifies when a young woman suddenly appears from behind the office and says something to her colleague sitting inside. Someone turns up the volume of the music, and the girl starts to dance again, this time like she was in a disco. She is staring at me the whole time, and I try to look the other way. She gives me strange looks as she sings along with the song. Suddenly, I realize she is not singing lyrics—she is singing to me. 'Hey! Hey you! Hey you over there! Hey there—Walid Dahman!'

I turn to look at her, 'Yes?'

'Stay … ! Stay right … ! Stay right where you are! We … ! We are … ! We are working on your case!'

She starts to dance again. I decide to get away from her and walk across the room, where I begin to pace back and forth. When I get bored with that, I stand in the middle of the room. As soon as the song stops, another one starts—yet the girl never takes a break from her dancing. I turn to look as far away from her as I can and my eyes catch sight of a small family sitting in a corner at the other end of the building. I see a man in his thirties, shaking an empty plastic water bottle. Next to him, a woman who is a bit younger, a girl maybe five years old, and a boy who is even younger. As they wait, they entertain each other by talking. Whatever they are talking about, it is clearly very Palestinian. When a soldier walks by, the man asks him if he might fill the bottle with water for the children. The politeness in his voice is embarrassing. The soldier agrees. The man's request awakens my own thirst. My thirst—it has been asleep all day and only now does it decide to wake up. My throat is as dry as a bone. My tongue sits like a hot stone in my mouth. The soldier comes back after filling the bottle with water and he gives it to the little girl who snatches it from his hands. I sit there watching the water pour into the girl's mouth. To me, it looks like a river flowing over a parched land. I try to swallow, but the only thing that goes down my throat is dryness. When the girl finishes drinking, she sets the bottle on the table in front of them. By now, I have lost my ability to go on looking without asking.

I walk over to the family and ask the man: 'How long have you all been waiting?'

'About two hours.'

He asks me to sit down and join them and I do not hesitate, since this was the very thing I was hoping he would ask. I learn from the man that he and his family live in Australia and have citizenship there. It took two days for them to fly here and this is their third day of travel. 'The trip from Sydney was not as exhausting as the wait at this crossing.'

I tell them a little about my trip, and a fleeting kind of friendship sparks between us—each of us a source of consolation for the VIP treatment we are now receiving. In a paradoxical way, the mistreatment of VIPs is a central strategy in the playbook by which the Israelis abuse all Palestinians, important or not. It is a special form of cruelty since its purpose is to puncture the delusion that the Oslo Accords could protect the importance of anybody.

I ask the man if I can have a drink and he hands me the bottle. What pours down my throat is the first liquid to pass through my lips since midnight yesterday.

My phone rings. It is my cousin, Abdelfettah. He tells me that he called Majda and that she has gone to get my mother's ID number. He also says that he contacted a Palestinian liaison officer on the other side of the crossing who promised that he would do everything he could to speed up my entry visa. I thank him for everything. Abdelfettah mentions that my mother has been calling him all day long, worrying about me. This last piece of news sends me into a tailspin—since I have no control over whether I will get through today. I tell Abdelfettah to tell my mother what he just told me, since it might reassure her to know that the PA is working on my behalf. I thank Abdelfettah and hang up.

Half an hour later, an Israeli soldier comes up to us and hands the family their documents. Ecstatic, they jump to their feet, not believing their good luck. The man and his wife wish me a speedy exit from this detention centre.

But my release does not arrive for a few more hours. At precisely 5.30 pm, the same first soldier to whom I had presented my papers now informs me that my visa will be ready in five minutes.

Precisely five minutes later, he brings me my passport. For some reason, he apologizes when he hands it to me. Without thinking about it, I thank him and leave.

I see three Palestinian workers walking toward a corridor of some sort and stop one to ask where I go to reach the Palestinian side. He tells me to follow them. I pull my suitcase behind me and struggle to keep up. We enter a wide tunnel whose end I cannot exactly see. The ceiling is arched, like a distant cement sky. The sound of our footsteps echoes back at us like the clomping of horses' hooves.

Stop. Lift up your shirt so we can see your chest.

I shall obey the voice calling out from a loudspeaker hidden somewhere above me in this vast, terrifying emptiness.

Turn around. Take one step forward. Go to room 2. It will push me through the metal bars into a twisting metal corridor from which I will emerge a broken man. Then I will rush to gather myself up again—but I will not regain my old shape and size until I come out of this cage again on my return to London.

After more than fifteen minutes, the end appears. I reach it by walking toward a plaza that spills onto a shapeless stretch of bare land.

I present my passport to one of the officers in the Palestinian Liaison office, and he seems to forget who I am. He records my name in the big 'Gaza Arrivals' register, then he hands it back to me.

I hear someone calling my name, 'Abu Fadi!' I turn to see who it is, and there is a lanky young man waving at me. He puts on his prescription glasses. Next to him are two others who are younger. The young man exclaims: 'So glad you got here safely, cousin! I'm Abdelfettah!'

I give the young man a big warm hug—I am genuinely happy to see him. He introduces me to his two brothers, Salah and Nasser, and I hug them in turn. Then the four of us pile into his car.

10

The car we ride in is a colourless old Fiat. The ride is bumpy, the asphalt is pockmarked, pitted, and littered with stones, wood and metal debris.

Salah, who sits directly behind me, tells me that the wasteland to the left used to be huge olive orchards until two years ago, when Israeli bulldozers ripped them out. There used to be tens of thousands of trees here. 'And part of that land used to be an orchard with the best citrus in all of Gaza.' We turn our heads and look when he says: 'The land on the right is what's left of the industrial park. That building, the one covered in soot whose name you can see—that's the Abu Galyun Tile Factory. That pile of rubble where you see the truck that's tipped over—that's what's left of the Falluji Soft Drink Company.' Salah tells us about how the entire industrial park was destroyed over six weeks during May and June 2003.

We veer to the right and climb a dirt berm covered with ruts and holes. As soon as we reach the level asphalt road on top, Beit Lahia looms at us like a hill rising from the centre of the earth.

Most of the buildings and homes on the edge of the city were destroyed. Abdelfettah tells me that Israeli tanks had advanced as far as that line before they had

had their fill of shelling the neighbourhood. The Israelis had stopped not less than fifty metres from their building, which sits right on the Beit Lahia–Jabalia line.

As soon as we settle onto the main road, my eyes behold the strangest sight. I can finally recognize Beit Lahia and Jabalia now. Long ago, these twin townships were shapeless, colourless piles of stone and wood and metal—the flotsam of a hurricane that opened up one night long ago and showered the land with shacks and tents. Like falling stars, these structures came crashing into the soil. Hurled down and thrown together—that was how these homes were formed, without recognizable shape or hue, without clear lines, lanes or streets, without any describable features at all. Yet there, amidst this massive pile of homes, grew a beautiful line of houses with a classical Arab style— arched windows like the old mansions of Damascus, like small mouths smiling down from the centre of the town's destruction. I could not understand how these homes had been spared the carnage. It looked like this housing development was somehow parachuted into Gaza from heaven itself.

'What is that?' I have to ask.

They tell me that this beauty smiling at us from the rubble is Sheikh Zayed City, built with aid from the United Arab Emirates. Apartments in the development were given to people who had been injured by the Israelis, or to the families of victims, and to those who had lost their homes during any of Israel's many incursions into the area. As our car drives by, I stare at these remarkable structures. I go on staring until my eyes fall upon an image of the nice sheikh himself.

We continue along, veering left then right. We come upon a vast stretch of rubble. Abdelfettah says that the houses that used to be there were bulldozed during the Israeli assault of September 2004.

We arrive at a side alley. Abdelfettah stops the car next to a huge poster affixed to the corner of the building directly in front of us. 'Abu Fadi, this is a memorial for your cousin Falah, God rest his soul.'

My eyes well up at the image of a young man who even in death, maintains a brave, warm smile. He looks like his father Nasreddine when he was that age—the same swarthy skin, the same dark hawk eyes, the same black hair. Falah was the exact image of his father, except for the fact that the occupation had torn it/him in half.

Abdelfettah drives, turns right and slips into another side alley. He pulls over and parks the car in front of a four-storey apartment house with a large iron door. I recognize it immediately: the Nasrite Building.

'Your mother's waiting for you upstairs,' Abdelfettah tells me. 'Be tough, Abu Fadi. It'll be fine.'

When I get to the last bachelor pad on the fourth floor, I find the door wide open, inviting me to set foot inside. Abdelfettah tells me to go in by myself while he and his brothers wait behind. 'Your mother insisted on being alone with you when you arrived. What she said was, "I want to get my fill of him before I have to share."'

Slightly afraid and hesitant, I step inside. I look around for the mother that the occupation took from me thirty-eight years earlier. I take a few steps into a foyer that seems to open onto a sitting room on the right. Then my eyes catch sight of the fringe of a thatch mat on the floor and the edges of rugs strewn about the hallway. I realize immediately where the sitting room is, and that my mother is somewhere inside.

Abdelfettah whispers something from where he is standing, reminding me to take off my shoes. I take a couple of last steps inside, turn to the right and my mother shrieks: 'Walid, my son! Welcome home, my beautiful son! I'm so glad you made it! I'm so glad to see you, my lovely, lovely son!'

My mother is sitting hunched over herself on a cotton mattress on the ground. She tries as best she can to get up, even if only to her knees—but I do not give her much of a chance. I bend down and bury my face in her shoulder, hugging her like the child I used to be. I kiss her and she begins to kiss me in return—once for every year I've been away. Then we sit and weep. We go on crying, saying nothing. The others outside let us bawl and bawl until our sniffles and snorts come to an end. Silently, they file into the room with looks of astonishment on their faces.

I sit right next to my mother. My hand clasps hers, just like it used to do when I was a child and she would drag me behind her on errands or visits to people's homes.

And I would go running along after her, sometimes clutching her hand, sometimes gripping her dress.

'Abu Fadi's here, Aunt!' Nasser cries.

'The brightness of your presence has lit up all Gaza, my son! This is the happiest day in my life—I've lived to see my boy after all these years! Welcome home, Walid! I'll say it a hundred times—welcome, welcome, welcome!' My mother begins to wipe her tears with the end of her headscarf, but the tears refuse to stop pouring. And I, the whole time, watch her face, looking for traces of the mother I knew.

After a while my cousin Nasreddine shuffles into the room, hauling all the years of his life on a cane. All his life, this man has made fun of the dark brown complexion of his skin. And now this man, whose arms were once made of steel, whose body was once that of a titan, is little more than an old man leaning over a walking stick.

Nasreddine—Abul-Abd—greets me warmly as he takes his shoes off at the end of the hallway. He begins to apologize for the way the years have treated him. 'I'm all messed up, cousin. As you can see, everything is either worn out or broken down.'

'As long as your odometer is still working, Abul-Abd, that's all that matters, right?'

Everyone laughs as he replies: 'That's the problem, cousin—the odometer is as busted as the motor!' I pull my hand from my mother's, and jump up to embrace Nasreddine. As we hug, we begin to cry. We continue to weep and embrace one another. As a youth, this man never wept—but now he does. He lightens our mood by recalling something we did as children, 'Remember Grandpa's goat, Walid? Remember when we took him out to graze in Beit Lahia forest and he ran away from us?'

He laughs and so do I, amidst all our tears. And suddenly I can see him again, the young man who used to carry his grandfather's goat across his shoulders like it was a kitten.

The sitting room begins to fill with well-wishers, with relatives I am meeting again after so many years, relatives who have grown up and whose faces I can no longer recognize. And relatives born long after I left—children of the occupation.

'Why were you so late, Abu Fadi? We kept getting ready to come over, but they'd call to tell us you still hadn't got here.'

'I got there at 9, but the crossing was closed. They said they caught a girl who was about to blow herself up.'

'Yeah. We saw it on TV,' my cousin Khaled interjects, then adds: 'As soon as the girl walked into the place where they do body cavity searches, they called out to her by name, "Take off your belt, Fida, and walk two steps forward." Her name's Fida al-Puss. The television said that she tried to detonate the explosive, but something malfunctioned. Then the soldiers grabbed her and now she's being detained.'

My cousin Abdel-Halim adds, 'Did you know, cousin—Fida al-Puss was the very last cat left in the Gaza Strip.'

Everyone around me bursts into laughter at the joke, but I sit there dumbfounded. Abdel-Halim tries to explain: 'Not so long ago, the PA launched an anti-rat campaign in Gaza. They put out packets of rat poison everywhere. The pussycats devoured the stuff and died. The rats didn't touch it—and now there are probably more rats than people here. And since the PA had its brilliant idea, there are no cats to catch them.'

'Sometimes curiosity really does kill the cat,' I reply, and everyone laughs.

Another relative joins in the conversation. 'Last week, a Palestinian from the West Bank came to visit his family in Gaza. The Israelis searched him at the crossing and found that he was carrying a kitten on his body. They took the animal away and warned the man: smuggling is strictly prohibited.'

As we laugh again, my cousin Abu Hatem walks in. Back when he was nine years old, I would send him out to buy Rothmans' cigarettes for me. I would bribe him with a penny or a falafel sandwich. Now the man is tall—much taller than I am. Here he stands before my eyes. For a while he says nothing, though on his lips plays a bright smile meant specially for me. Meanwhile, all eyes are on us—he and I were the closest of all to one another. In an instant, I am on my feet. I stand there staring in disbelief—that little boy is now a distinguished-looking man in his fifties. He is as handsome and neat as his father was. We rush to embrace each other, shouting.

They make space for him and he sits down by my side. Before he has finished drying his tears, he bellows: 'What did I miss? What were you talking about before I got here?'

'We were talking about the al-Puss girl who held me up at the crossing.'

'Hey—let's just be grateful she didn't blow herself up, otherwise we wouldn't have seen you at all today. Welcome, cousin—glad to see you safe and sound.'

As we talk, one of my relatives hands me a small piece of paper and whispers: 'This is the public statement that the girl's family issued.'

I snatch the paper from his hand. What I read is astounding and infuriating. It also makes me want to cry all over again. In the statement, Fida's family named the organizations that sent their daughter to do it, and they also explained that their daughter is mentally ill and prone to suicide attempts. They said that the Israelis had made arrangements for their daughter to be treated at a hospital in Israel. Because of this, Fida had papers that allowed her to go through the Erez crossing regularly. When they discovered this, Hamas and Fatah wanted to exploit it. The family said that the Israelis had been kinder to their daughter than the people who had tried to use her today.

I fold up the paper and go to the room that Abdelfettah showed me. The room is all prepared for me—my cousins have even delivered my suitcase there. I slip the statement into my backpack as quickly as possible, then go back to sit with the others. One of them speaks up and surprises me by telling me something even worse than what I just read. 'You know, it was one of your cousins who sent Fida to blow herself up at the crossing.'

'One of my cousins?'

'Yes—Hussein al-Hajj Khalil Dahman. Hussein is in the al-Aqsa Brigades. He's the one in charge of coordinating operations with Hamas. And people are already saying that this was a joint action between them.'

I had never before heard of a Dahman picking up a weapon. Never heard of one of us killing someone. None of us ever joined the military back during Egyptian rule. None of us ever joined the Palestinian liberation army either. Yet now I begin to hear that fourteen Dahmans gave their lives during the Second Intifada. And now the Dahmans have taken up arms. Some of us even staged an armed demonstration in front of the Legislative Council, demanding that a certain execution order be carried out. That has to do with the story of how my cousin Hussein's brother, Hani, was murdered by a fellow officer in the Preventive Security Force where Hani worked. Dahmans staged another demonstration, demanding that the PA investigate the assassination of Yasser Dahman who taught at the Islamic University. He was killed by an explosive that had been placed in his office at the university, and the family wanted the killers to be brought to justice. I learn that Abu Ahmad, my mother's cousin, lost his oldest son three years ago. The ten-year-old boy was playing with other kids when he was run over by an Israeli tank.

I go to sleep at about 2 in the morning. I have not been asleep for more than an hour when I am woken by the sounds of dozens of muezzins. Their calls clash and jumble over one another, like a band of musicians warming up before a concert. I mutter to myself and try to go back to sleep. But not half an hour goes by when the calls begin again, now even louder and more cacophonous. It is as if these are not real muezzins, but trainees who have been told to practise all night long. *What the hell? Are Gazans now required to perform dawn prayers twice?*

Later the next evening, I pose this question to my cousin, sheikh Sobhi, who is an imam steeped in all things Islamic. He answers in the classical Arabic that he believes raises his stature in the eyes of others: 'What thou heardst at the outset was the invitation to rise. This was not the call to prayer that thou knowst well, but rather an invitation to rise and prepare for the call. And he who wouldst go forth to pray, let him to the mosque nearest his abode.'

'What? At 3 in the morning? So when do people sleep?'

'The call that follows is the call to prayer proper.'

But in fact, with so many muezzins, the space between 'the invitation' and 'the call' gets filled with recitations and prayers. There is literally no audible space—no silence—between the two.

Just before sunrise, I almost get back to sleep when I am roused again, this time by a rooster. The last time I heard a cock crow was years ago—and that was in an old Egyptian soap opera. My eyes open and I can do nothing but laugh. The crow of a live—not prerecorded—rooster is simply amazing to hear. The bird's swagger is so beautiful and melodious, he is the perfect metaphor for the kind of leaders Palestinians have enjoyed over the years. I imagine the rooster stretching out his body as tall as he can, spreading out his legs, proudly filling himself up with breath, as if air was a spirit that filled his insides to their utmost. He extends his wings and feathers as widely as possible, till his body is bigger than its actual size. Then he unfurls his tail feathers like a peacock strutting over a field of competitors. He raises his head, and his bright red comb goes stiff like a royal crown. And he stays there like that until he decides that the time to rise is at hand and then, for the sake of every hen within earshot, he belts out his warning against those who would still sleep.

I am happy to be here. To be hearing this. But within seconds, my sense of contentment comes to an end, scattered in the darkness of the bedroom by the symphony of dozens of other roosters in the camp who return the rooster's good deed. They begin to challenge the first rooster, letting it be known that they too have kept vigil all night, watching over the alleys of the camp, and hinting that they would have been the first to crow had not their biological clocks been set to slightly different shades of time. Like the muezzins, these roosters have not agreed to set their clocks to the same hour.

On the roof directly over my head, great celebrations begin—like the shouting festivals of one of the armed factions. As soon as the roosters' festival starts, here and there on the roof a clucking or two begins as well. At first it is hushed, like a timid confession: 'Ka-ka-ka-bak-bak-bak-baak.' This is followed by a mass chirping, then the cluckings that grow louder and stormier like the singing of men at a wedding—right at that moment when they take the groom off their shoulders and set him down at his door. They stomp on the ground with some envy, but mostly to encourage him to accomplish the heroic feat now facing him. And they sing loudly as they push in the door. Above my head, the hens continue their chorus: 'Bak-bak-bak-bak, bak-bak-bak-bak !'

The chickens across the camp now fill the night air with their screeching din. People tolerate this carnival only because of the thousands of eggs they lay every morning.

I lie there awake for a long while, watching as the morning swaps its cloak of darkness for a glittering silver robe. When my eyes have had their fill of wakefulness, I do not resist. I go back to sleep, forgetting all the morning events soon to come. I drift off, barely mindful of the sound of car engines and the donkey-driven vegetable carts that create a particular kind of racket whose tone I had successfully repressed decades ago. I half listen to the hammering of carpenters and the pounding of metal workers which announce the start of another working day. And there, among the other sounds, I can still hear the buzzing of an Israeli drone whose whine never stopped once the whole night.

My first morning home is epileptic—I can neither sleep, nor am I awake.

11

That morning, I greet my mother with a kiss on her forehead that I have been waiting to give her for decades. She responds by saying that now that I am here she can relax, knowing she will be happy for the rest of her days. When I sit down next to her, she asks whether I slept well.

I tell her that I closed my eyes for about two hours. I go on telling her about the ridiculous events, explaining how I was hounded by the barking of dogs. Unlike English canines that abide by anti-barking laws, Palestinian dogs have no compunction about breaking the law. I tell her how the crowing of roosters had taught me that the dawn belongs to them alone, and not to the muezzins who cannot agree with one another on a singing work schedule. I talk about how lively and snappy the nocturnal gunfire is. 'The hens, Mama—the hens! They must be the only workers in the world who meet all their production quotas before the sun comes up. And the braying of donkeys, Mama. I haven't heard such a sweet, gentle sound in many, many years. I miss the braying of donkeys, Mama! Such patriotic donkeys Gaza has!'

My mother says nothing. She bites her lip, unsure what to say. I add: 'You know, Mama, we have absolutely no donkeys where I live. If someone were to bring one to London, I bet they'd want to put it in the zoo, or on display somewhere. And then the media would rush around to cover it—it'd be a huge event. Tourists would pull out their cameras to take photos of themselves standing next to the donkey as a souvenir of the miraculous occasion. They'd take the beast on tour around the whole country. They'd establish an official pedigree for him and his asinine ancestors and give him an annual physical. You know, I was sort of hoping that someone might take a picture of me standing next to a Palestinian donkey. And don't get me going about all the carts that the night farts out of its arse. Mama, don't be shocked by how I talk—you use the same expression. And the call to prayer—God damn the call to prayer in this country! As if my ears weren't sore enough from having to listen to Israeli soldiers shout and yell all day. Aren't five hundred muezzins screeching into five hundred microphones a bit much? Has the Resurrection Day come early for Gazans? Are people so afraid for their place in heaven? Why don't they get themselves into a neat single-file line and wait until their cases come up for review? It's a pity that each muezzin trusts only his personal timepiece.'

My mother begins to laugh, then stops herself.

'For forty years, Mama, the various Palestinian factions have never joined together in a single front. So why would I expect Palestinian muezzins to form a unified front during my visit?'

My mother banishes the traces of an unlaughed laugh. When she talks, her voice is gentle and reassuring. 'Don't worry about it, son. That was only your first night back home. By tomorrow you'll be used to it again. Between you and me, we stopped noticing these things long ago. We don't notice anything any more. We sleep through artillery barrages. It is like nothing happened—that's how used to it we are. You want to know how fucked up life is here? I'll tell you. When it is completely quiet and there's not a sound outside— that's when I get so nervous I can't sleep.

'Get up, my good son—go and shave, take a hot shower. You'll start to wake up and feel more rested. Amal is going to come over and bring us our breakfast. Get yourself ready, your cousin Maryam called a little while ago and said she was going to stop by. She wants to see you. Maryam's crazy about you, you know. Get up and get ready.'

*

Two women in their early sixties walk into the last bachelor pad. They walk down the short hallway and stop near the mattress on the floor. As they remove their shoes, they greet my mother and look at me. Four eyes watch me with great curiosity.

I get up to welcome them, genuine warmth and inquisitiveness on my part too. I hold out my hand to each of them. We sit down, a small circle around my mother who, as usual, sits hunched over herself on the ground. Not for one moment does she stop welcoming the women into the room.

The first one looks at me. She is very dark-skinned. With a warm, friendly smile, she says, 'Of course you remember me, right, Abu Fadi? I'm your cousin, Maryam.'

'Umm Zahir,' my mother adds.

'Maryam?'

I lean over and embrace her, our eyes filled with tears. Maryam, my cousin, was a few years younger than me. Unlike her brother Nasreddine, who made fun of and cursed his complexion, Maryam loved the pigment of her skin, just as others in the family also loved it—she had a classic, Pharaonic kind of beauty. My mother had once wanted me to marry her brother's daughter. And, whenever the thought occurred to her, she didn't hesitate to talk about it at length. 'Walid, Maryam is as dark and sweet as a black plum. She's got a great sense of humour, and her lips almost drip with honey. And you know, she is sweet on you. She likes you. I swear to God, she once told me, "Where am I going to find someone as good as my cousin?"'

And I used to answer: 'Mama, Maryam is beautiful and sweet, and every cousin would love to marry her, but now's not the right time. I still have to finish my studies. I've got my future and the path before me is still a long one. When it's time to get married, God will give her away, and each of us will take his share of what fate has in store for him.'

Maryam, this Nefertiti of a woman, makes me forget the other woman who's come with her, whose name I still do not know. Eventually, Maryam notices that while I am studying the other woman, she is stealing sly looks at me. She rushes to correct things. 'Abu Fadi, this is my neighbor Leila. Leila's a distant relative, by the way. She's the daughter of al-Hajj Hassan Darwish who used to live in Jabalia Camp West. She's lived with her husband's family ever since they were married. She lives right next door to me in Khan Yunis.'

Something inside me begins to stir. I cannot tell whether I have fallen into a dream, or am waking from one. There is something about Leila. She awakens my senses and confounds them too. This is Leila from my novel—the Leila that Adel El-Bashity fell in love with decades ago. The Leila that Adel returned to find. The Leila that I, following in his footsteps, hoped to find for both of us. Has she stepped out of the text to welcome me home?

The two women say goodbye and get up to go. Maryam walks out of the apartment, and with her, a real Leila.

12

We are a society of gossips, of chitchat as twisted as those slogans we repeat and repeat until we begin to think they are fact. We are a people convinced that our blather pierces through fog and strikes at the heart of the grandest truths of all. On the afternoon of my second day, I am instantly immersed in all this chatter, and I cannot find my way out again until the very end of the evening. This is the daytime version of the night-time chaos that has kept me awake. Every last relative comes to welcome me, some of them to meet me for the first time. They have all heard so much about the only author the Dahmans ever produced. They are all impressed by the three novels he has written. They have seen him a few times on television, gesticulating wildly with his hands as he expertly discusses literature and politics, using the kinds of words some people get and some do not. And when they see their cousin the journalist, it gives them real pleasure to exchange glowing praise and knowing looks with one another. 'That's Walid—he's our cousin.' It is entirely possible that some have come only out of respect for my mother. Or perhaps *respect* is not the right word. It could be that they *fear* those broadcasts of hers that continue round the clock, except during those very early morning hours when she is sleeping. And even then, it is possible that her updates continue unabated in special dream coverage. She would not hesitate to ruin the reputation of a person who failed to arrive in a timely fashion to wish her well on the safe arrival of a son who had been absent for such an unprecedented amount of time.

The relatives continue to throng to the last bachelor pad whose sitting room, for this event, we have amply furnished with stuffed cotton mattresses and pillows for everyone to sit on. And meanwhile, my mother keeps repeating: 'See, Walid. The son of Sofia, your father's aunt, still has not bothered to come. Oh, he says he's sorry, *My son's getting married*. So what? Go marry off your son for all I care. Who could get mad at you for doing that? God help the man and help his bride. I hope the two of them give birth to a barnful of boys and girls.

'But still, what's so hard about coming over to greet your cousin? Couldn't you at least come over before your son's wedding to say hello to an old woman whose son has just returned? The bride's not going to run away, is she? The earth isn't going to open up and swallow her, is it? The wedding's tomorrow—if he doesn't come to see us, we're not going to attend. It's as simple as that. If someone doesn't come to see you, it's not right for you to visit them—no matter if all the kids in their family were getting married on the same day. Am I right, or am I wrong?'

My cousin Abul-Abd interrupts her. 'Don't be like that, Aunt. You know as well as I do what a pain a wedding can be. I married off five of my kids. Nowadays, people are so busy they don't even have time to scratch their head when it itches.'

My mother is not convinced—she begins to complain about how there are others who have also not shown up. And she starts to rattle off their names one by one. And for each person on the list, she swears an oath that she is never going to speak to them again.

Emad tries to change the subject by bringing up an old joke – one so good, he swears, that he is sure I could not have heard it before. It is about an electronic device made in Korea, and an operation to implant it under my mother's tongue. It was supposed to operate by remote control, but unfortunately, the device did not work so well. 'I've been pressing the stop button this whole time, but it's not responding.'

I laugh and my mother joins in, even as she wastes no time trying to show how wrong the remote control theory is. She tells everybody that it has been forty years since she sat with her son, and that she is going to say everything she has kept inside her all these years. 'Whoever wants to listen can do so. And whoever doesn't, can stick a finger in their ears. And whoever needs a device can go implant one in themselves.'

More than a couple of people in the room protest. 'Don't take it so hard, we don't mean it. Go ahead and speak.'

Like an Israeli helicopter in the Gaza sky, my mother relaxes as soon as she realizes that she is in total control of the situation—and she seizes the opportunity to talk even more.

Abu Ahmad, my mother's cousin who is a fervent Hamas supporter, steps in to change the direction of the conversation. 'The men from Hamas have acquired anti-tank mines. I saw them planting some with my own eyes. I even saw them detonate one.'

He addresses his words to Abu Khalil, the cousin sitting next to him, who has been worn down by an unrequited devotion to Fatah all these years.

Abu Khalil is not having any of it. 'You're making that up.'

'No, I saw one—it was an actual mine. Why is it so hard to believe, Abu Khalil? I'm telling you, it was an anti-tank explosive. I saw the cloud of dirt that went up when they detonated it under the tank. There was a plume of smoke and dust all across the sky. What do you expect our men to do? Plant mines and then put up warning signs that say: *Danger, you are now approaching a Hamas minefield!*'

'Abu Ahmad, my friend, what are you talking about? I am sure that the explosion you saw wasn't any bomb. And Hamas doesn't have any mines to plant anywhere. What you saw was most probably just a truck hitting a wall. That would raise the cloud of dust you think you saw. If I'm wrong, then tell me this—where did the tank go when it got hit by the mine?'

'The Jews came and towed it away.'

'May God come and tow away both your tongues!' my mother says. When my mother intervenes, she is like a multinational force parachuting into a conflict zone. And by the time she gets there, the conflict is done. Abu Ahmad and Abu Khalil swallow their tongues.

Confident that no one will interrupt her as long as she is talking to her long-lost son, my mother continues, 'Abu Fadi, you don't want to go on listening to Abu Ahmad and Abu Khalil's tall tales, do you? Those two do nothing but fight whenever they meet. And their fight is nothing but words. One of them stands over in Hamas' corner, the other stands up to defend Fatah. And each heaps insults on the other. Listen to your mother—and don't pay any attention to what they say. It's nonsense. And about that ring—I held on to it for over a year. Then I placed it with Ansam, your niece, for safekeeping. God rest her mother's soul.'

She wipes away two sudden tears with a handkerchief, and continues. 'It cost two hundred dollars. You know who gave me the money? Your sister, Raja, God rest her soul. I go to my neighbour Majda. You know Majda— you and your cousin were calling her from the crossing to see if she could go to the house in Khan Yunis and get you my ID number. I give her five hundred dollars and I tell her: "Listen, Majda, my dear, go buy some gold with this money." Gold is always better to have than dollars. Besides, I don't even have a bank account. Everyone else puts their money in bank accounts, don't they?'

I catch Emad's eye and cry out for help: 'Someone, hand me the remote! Please!'

While everyone laughs, Abu Ahmad seizes the chance to launch another attack on his political opponent. 'You know, Abu Khalil, your neighbour Shehada wanted to become a government minister. They wanted to make him Minister of Health, you know.'

'Screw them! What the hell does Shehada know about health, anyway? Here is what our neighbour knows about health: when he gets a headache, he stays home from work. He sits in bed and takes off a week's worth of sick days.'

'You think that the other guys who became ministers are any better than him?'

'Look, cousin, maybe—maybe—he could handle things at the Ministry of Sewage.'

Everybody is cracking up again, when Abul-Abd jumps in. 'So sewage gets its own PA ministry now? Is that why it stinks so bad?'

Abu Khalil's enthusiasm grows as the conversation goes on—and he adds: 'Look, old man. The Jews came to the PA and said: "We would like to purchase your sewage." And the PA told them: "No." So the Jews came back begging, and this time they didn't pose their request in that garbled Hebrew they speak. This time they asked in clear, comprehensible Arabic: "We will pay good money for your shit." But still the PA refused to sell. They said the Jews were going to collect it and treat it and turn it into gold. Pure gold, my friend. And the Jews went on saying: "Please let us take it off your hands."'

Abu Ahmad cuts him dead. He is so upset you might think we had been talking about selling the nation's soul. 'You mean they're trying to get it on the cheap, cousin?'

'Hand over that long beard of yours—you don't deserve to wear one! You're deluded if you think Israel would pay cash for your shit. The PA never once was so deluded to suppose that a country could sell its citizens' shit for hard cash. Not even the EU pays cash for shit— and they pay cash for everything around here. Israel merely made an offer to purchase, that's all. First in shekels, then in dollars, if you must know. Does that sound like a good deal to you?'

Abu Ahmad is now defiant. 'No, I do not like it one bit. First of all, the sewage project is German. The engineer overseeing it is German. And he said they're going to use it to irrigate the lands to the west of Beit Lahia. If the faeces is sold, our German friend is going to be disappointed. And don't tell me that he belongs to Hamas—or have Germans gone and joined the Islamic resistance now?'

'The sewer project? You think that's really going to happen?'

'Do you think these things can be done overnight? Sheikh Zayed City in Jabalia stood unfinished for years. The construction was stopped for years until Mahmoud Abbas came in.'

'What are you talking about? Abbas was in Egypt at the time. The PA has refused to sell the sewage. They have even said so publicly, *We will not sell our shit to Israel*. They want to treat it and reclaim it just like they do in developed countries. The PA is on public record as saying: *This crap belongs to the nation and we're not going to treat it like shit. We will not let anyone shit on the excrement of the good people of Jabalia and Beit Lahia*. The PA considers excrement a non-negotiable part of national sovereignty, and would never compromise on the issue without a general referendum. They did pretty much everything they could have done on the issue. Although I guess they could have organized public demonstrations. I can hear it now—crowds of patriots in Jabalia and Beit Lahia shouting:

It's our shit, now get in line
Us in front and you behind!
Our shit, our shit, friend or foe
Belongs to us, for evermore!'

'And what happened in the end?' I interrupt, hoping to put an end to this crappy conversation.

'Ho!' Abu Khalil answers. 'The PA came and the PA went—but the shit never left, did it? The whole area reeks of it. You smell it wherever you go. The sewers are overflowing. And don't forget that Gaza's sewers pour directly into the sea. And Wadi Gaza too—it is now nothing but a canyon of pipes pumping the nation's shit into the Mediterranean. And the water supply is polluted, so now we have to buy bottled water from the Jews.'

Amal, Abdelfettah's wife, brings out cups of coffee, followed by cups of tea. Everyone sits and drinks as much as they like, shifting their bodies back and forth now and then. Their legs get tired, even though they're used to sitting this way.

Well-wishers keep on coming and going. The conversation never stops, nor does my mother's broadcast system. There is no remote control in the world that could stop her now—not even one made by Sony. No one listens to anyone else. Abu Ahmad locks horns with Abu Khalil and their private battle goes on. My mother tells me stories and I am somehow expected to listen to all channels at the same time and follow each of their many updates. I am supposed to take in and comment on everything that is said in my capacity as professional journalist or television guest brought in to comment, as an outsider.

It is another day of incredible, laughable and heart-breaking reunions. I let them go on saying whatever they want to say. I jump in sometimes with a word or two, simply to let them know I am still listening. But that is never enough for my mother—she insists on dragging me into things with that tongue, and I let myself be dragged along by her. 'I'll tell you what's a fact—when I hear someone is a Hamas supporter, I turn my back on them. If they walk by, I don't say hello.

When the Israelis kill someone, those jerks run around everywhere making such a racket about it. And then they try to give money to the poor victim's family. In other words, if I can be blunt with you—they're buying people, that's what they're trying to do. Am I right or am I wrong?'

'Auntie, you're absolutely right,' Salah ventures.

'I know how to talk politics better than the lot of you.' And, for the first time, my mother stops talking.

13

It is almost midnight when the last well-wishers leave the last bachelor pad and my mother and I are by ourselves again, just as we were in the morning.

She asks if I want to sleep, and I tell her that I am worn out and need at least twenty hours of sleep. But, even so, I do not feel like going to bed right away.

I lean toward her until my shoulder is touching hers. Before I say anything, she asks, 'What's bothering you, son? I know there's something. I'm your mother—you can't hide anything from me, Walid.'

'How long have you known Leila Dahman, Mama?'

'Leila Dahman? What made you think of her right now?'

'I'm just asking.'

'Well, I've known her ever since she was a girl. She's only a couple of years younger than you, and she is a cousin of ours. She's not a distant relative, you know. Why are you asking about her?'

'It's just that ... did she ever marry?'

'You think a woman like that would be left unmarried? God forbid! A woman as beautiful as the moon not finding a husband? No, no, no—not when any hag in this town can expect to find a ring on her finger! What are you trying to insinuate?'

My mother turns and looks away. As far away as she can, as if she wants to hide the expression that is on her face. She is just like me. Her face always betrays what she is feeling. She shifts in her seat and places her right hand onto her knee, then rests her chin on her fist. Then she falls into a silence that is, for her, completely unnatural.

I cannot stand her silence, and I decide to chase after it. 'OK. So then why didn't Leila come with her husband? He must be family too, right? Shouldn't he have come with her to greet me?'

She shifts again, putting her left hand on her other knee. Now I can see her face. The sadness and gloom are as clear as day. She pauses for a moment, before relinquishing the silence. 'Leila was married to her cousin Waddah. He was an exceptional young man— as handsome as she is beautiful. He was so upstanding that when people in Khan Yunis went to utter a serious oath, they did it on his name. His death was a complete shock. No one expected anything like it. One morning, he's going to work, he's walking out the front door, he's shutting the door behind him. And then all of a sudden, he's struck in the head by a bullet. No one ever found out whether it was the Jews or those armed men who run around in the street all day long.'

She stops and looks at me. Then, her tone even more grave, asks: 'Now I've told you. So you tell me. Why are you so interested in her? I know you are. You can't hide it. Have you got your eye on Leila now? Does that mean you're thinking about divorcing Jala?'

'Julie, Mama. My wife's name is Julie.'

'Jala, Julu—it's all the same.'

My legs are sore from sitting so long, so I stretch them out in front of me. Reassuring her, I say, 'The man who's divorced his wife is someone else, Mama. It's a Palestinian man who knew Leila when she was young, back in high school. A young man from the Bashity family. From Majdal-Asqalan, who lives in Germany now. His name is Adel. He contacted me, asking about her. He was going to visit Gaza and he wanted to find out where she was— but didn't want to go around asking about her himself. He didn't want people talking about her. Even though it's an old story, you know how people can be.'

'You think Leila would have fallen in love with someone from Majdal? No way! The girl was always such a prude.'

'Mama, I don't have to tell you that young people know how to keep a secret.'

'OK, clever clogs. Who are you still in love with then?'

'This isn't about me. Let's stick to the subject of Leila.'

'Kids can be stupid—and that was a long time ago. Why is your friend thinking about Leila all of a sudden?'

'He was married to a German woman for ten years. Then the marriage fell apart. He divorced her and that was that. They had one daughter, and she married an American and emigrated to New York with him. Every so often, he'd call home and ask about Leila. When he heard that her husband died, he thought of going back. He wants to spend the rest of his life with a Palestinian woman. And he and Leila were once in love with one another.'

My mother sits up like she is just waking up from a dream, 'Listen. Listen. Maybe your friend is thinking about another Leila who also used to live in Jabalia Camp West. That Leila died though.'

'Who died?'

'Sheikh Khalil Dahman's daughter—Leila Dahman. Her story is sad too. Her husband also died, you know. In a shoot-out between Fatah and Hamas, two years ago. He didn't have anything to do with either faction, of course. The poor woman joined him in the grave two months later. People said she got stomach cancer from all the lead pollution and all the Israeli airstrikes. Who knows? Cancer's all over the Gaza Strip. So many people have cancer now. Some of them get treatment at Hadassah Hospital in Jerusalem. Some go to Ramallah. Others don't get any treatment at all—God help them. And then—'

'Mama, you said her husband got shot during a clash between the factions, and not by a stray bullet, right?'

'That's right. Though some put the blame on—'

Before my mother finishes, I interrupt her: 'I'm going to bed, Mama. Sleep well.'

So the Leila who came with my cousin is the Leila that Adel's looking for.

'What did you just say, son?'

'Nothing, Mama. I'll tell you later. Sleep well.'

'You too, my love. Sleep tight, Walid.'

I head to my bedroom and let my mother tell the rest of her stories to herself.

I lie down on the bed, exhausted from another day of meeting people and listening to strange and agonizing stories. These tales raced ahead of me and folded themselves in the sheets. They're all here, waiting to retell themselves, detail by detail.

After a while, I get up and turn off the lights, go back to bed and close my eyes. I try to go to sleep, but I cannot. The story of Adel keeps me wide-awake. I'd made the story up for my novel but now key elements have begun to appear as facts in the stories my mother tells. In the shapeless gloom of this room, I watch as Leila steps out of my novel and takes her seat on the edges of reality.

I begin to regret the day I consigned the story of Leila to fiction. I had been thinking this whole time that it was something made up by a stranger. By a random person who wrote to me at the newspaper to tell me how much he liked my column. And to ask me for help. Now I regret that I jumped to the conclusion I did.

It was about a year ago when I got the email.

Dear Mr Dahman,

First, permit me to introduce myself to you. I am a fellow Palestinian. Exile has consumed half of my life, just as it has yours. When I was young, I knew a beautiful girl from your family. Her name was Leila Dahman, and I am pretty sure she is a relative of yours. We used to meet on the sly, back in Jabalia Camp. When night began to fall, we would talk to one another. During the day it was something else. We never did more than smile at one another from afar when I was walking home from school. I fell in love with Leila, and I have never felt the same way about any other woman in my life. I can honestly say that there's never been anybody I've loved but her. Leila and I vowed to marry one day. But I left to study in Germany, thinking I would return when I graduated. I never did get to come back. As my life slipped away from me, so did Leila. Years ago, I learned that Leila finally married someone. But recently I found out that her husband passed away. I do not know where she is or how to find her. Every effort I've made to contact her has failed. And it is to ask for your help that I have come to you. As a well-connected journalist and writer, your ties to your family must be strong. I hoped you might be able to help me to find Leila. If you do manage to find her for me, I will personally go to Gaza to ask for her hand in marriage, even though I am almost sixty years old. If fate decides against me and she rejects my proposal, I will, of course, respect her wishes.

The poor man signed off by writing his mobile number and two lines of poetry that harked back to that epitome of that hopeless mad lover, Qays, who—like this man—

had once lost his heart and mind to a woman named Leila:

> I love Leila passionately, the way the soul loves,
>   and Love is a seducer!
> O Exile of the heart, among the sons of the Dahman
>   you shall find her!

I was stunned by the nerve of the man to ask me to help him in such a private matter—and one that concerned someone I did not even know. At the time, I did not take his story at all seriously. It was so strange—if it were true, it would only mean he was desperate and somewhat mad. It would raise suspicions to go around asking about a woman—a widow, no less! So I was not going to do it. Besides, how did he expect me to go asking around when it would only uncover the kind of old relationship that her family would hold against her? And what would the dead husband's family think if they found out? If Adel wanted this done, he should go to Gaza himself and do it. Or was he smart enough to realize that he would be beaten to a pulp for asking? That may be why he wanted me to do it for him. The whole thing was probably a practical joke.

I wrote back to Adel and let him know that I was not willing to play matchmaker for him, or to stumble around in the dark looking for his lost bride. I told him to travel to Gaza and look for his old flame himself— that is, if she really ever existed.

Later, as time went by, I found myself using the story in the email as I began working on my novel. All I had was a premise for a story: after a long absence, a Palestinian exile returns to Gaza by way of Israel. The novel was going to be about how everything has changed in the years he has been gone.

At the time, I was just beginning the novel and had not yet got into the details. When I began to write, I made this fellow—Adel El-Bashity—into the protagonist, and made him take the advice I had given to the real Adel El-Bashity who had written to me. He goes to Gaza and searches for Leila. And it was only later, at my wife's suggestion, that I decided to go to Gaza to retrace the steps that Adel takes in his journey—and to reflect on the hardships he would experience in his story.

And that is how I now find myself walking in Adel's shoes—searching out Leila, for him and also for me. Looking for her in the novel and in the story I am living. Following her through the shadow of fiction and in the light of fact.

Remembering all this gives me a sense of relief, and begins to make up for all the sleep I have lost. I turn the lights back on and connect my laptop to the phone socket. When I open my email, I find four new messages waiting for me. The first is an advertisement for penis enlargements. I laugh to myself as I hit delete. *No thank you—it's fine just the way it is*. The second email is about a credit card, so I ignore it. The third is from my friend Leah Portman, telling me she's just come back from Germany and that her tour there has been a success from what she could tell.

The fourth email is a surprise. It is from Dana. I read it, not fully believing that this woman actually carried through on her promise to write to me.

Hi Walid.

I enjoyed meeting you. I hope you have arrived safely and been able to see your mother by now. I've been worrying about you since hearing about the bomber who tried to blow herself up at Erez. Are you OK?

Dana

I dash off a reply to Dana. I tell her that it has been a moving experience to see my mother again, that it has been intense and nerve-racking but also very beautiful. Being with family is like swimming in a deep sea of warmth and love. I thank her for thinking of me, and encourage her to hold onto her views about peace. Then I shut the computer, flick off the lights and get into bed again. I have no idea when I finally fall asleep.

14

'Your cousin Abu Hatem is coming over in the after-noon,' my mother tells me as we finish breakfast. 'He's going to take you to Khan Yunis just like he promised.'

Thus begins my third morning.

'He's taking you off to Khan Yunis even though I haven't been able to spend any time with you yet, Walid. Don't go off and stay too long. Maybe a day or two, and then come right back, OK?'

'We still have a lot of time, Mama.' I try to reassure her while I clear the dishes. After setting the dishes in the kitchen, I tell my mother I am going to go up onto the roof to see the view and catch a breath of fresh air.

Over on one side of the roof stand the cages—from which the chickens and pigeons trumpet their pre-crepuscular greetings. I walk over to the low wall on the southern side of the building where I see a Palestinian flag wrapped around a wooden pole. It looks as if a whirlwind has twisted the cloth around itself until it choked. I unravel it, then hold it out by a corner. As I let go, it begins to snap and breathe in the wind.

I stand there, my eyes wandering over the view of Jabalia and Beit Lahia. I look at the large open space between the Nasrite Building and the next one, to the west. I spy green and yellow and black flags fluttering here and there on the different buildings, each proclaiming the sympathies of inhabitants inside. The flag I used to salute is nowhere to be found among them.

Off to the north, behind a patch of empty land, I can just see some houses surrounded by a sparse thicket of trees. When I squint, I can make out the faint outlines of a tall mast—*a radio antenna in Dugit, probably*.

I breathe in the cool morning air and take out my mobile phone. Half sitting on the low wall, I dial the number I received in the email from more than a year ago.

'Hello, is this Adel El-Bashity?'

'Yes, it is. Who's calling?'

'Adel, it's Walid Dahman. Do you remember—'

'Of course! Walid, the journalist? *Mein Gott!* Where have you been all this time?'

'Good morning, Adel.'

'My God. I suspect you have something to tell me, otherwise you wouldn't be calling.'

'Adel—how soon can you come to Gaza?'

'Where are you calling from, Walid?'

'Jabalia.'

'Really? I'm in Gaza right now myself. I arrived here three days ago.' He is almost shouting into the phone. 'I thought I was playing it safe to come through Egypt. Then I got stranded at Rafah for five days. Don't ever go there. It's nothing but sweltering heat and mosquitoes, and garbage and crowds. Screeching crowds. I've never been to hell, but I'm sure the entrance to it is nicer than the Rafah crossing.'

'Listen, I need to tell you some news, but I want to tell you in person. Could we meet?'

'Yes! I'm ready any time. Yours truly has nothing to keep him occupied.'

'Let's meet outside the Andalus Hotel at noon. How's that?'

'Perfect. I'll see you then.'

'Wait a second—how will we recognize one another?'

'I have a copy of *Jasmine Alley* with me. I read most of it on the plane and in Rafah. I'll be carrying the novel in my hand. And anyway, don't forget—your picture is on the back cover.'

'Right—see you then.'

I hang up, not believing that I am going to meet the real Adel, a man I have never seen in real life. He might just end up pushing the other Adel out of my novel.

I fly down the stairs to the apartment.

We arrive at the hotel at the same time, and take a small table next to a window overlooking the sea. We sit across from one another. For the first time, there we are—me and Adel El-Bashity, face to face.

Adel is completely different from the Adel in my novel. He is tall and broad-shouldered. His moustache blends into a closely cropped beard, the kind everyone seems to wear these days.

Deep worry casts a shadow over his good looks. If I wanted to, I could put an end to his anxiety with two quick words. But instead, I decide to let him go on spilling his guts onto our little table. I ask him to update me on the latest developments in his search for Leila.

The waiter brings Adel a cup of coffee, and a cup of tea with mint for me. Adel sips his coffee while looking out at the sea, as if he might find refuge there. Finally, he turns to me and says, 'All my efforts have sadly come to naught. I wish you had agreed to help when I asked. You would have spared me a lot of trouble.'

'What happened?'

'What happened? You tell me. On the phone, you implied that you had some good news for me. Can I hear what it is?'

'Not until I hear what you've been through.'

'Fine. I drove myself crazy looking for Leila. You know how touchy the issue is to begin with. Some strange man comes from Europe asking everybody about a fifty-year-old widow. And what I found out in the end was this. Some people told me that Leila died of cancer some time ago, but they couldn't tell me where she was buried. Others told me that she was still alive, but they don't know where she lives. I am exhausted and cannot go on like this. The people who say she's dead can't direct me to her grave. The people who insist she's still alive can't point me to where she lives. My Leila's lost between two unknown addresses—one above ground, the other below—but I can't find either. So here I am, still looking.'

I laugh.

'Are you making fun of me, Walid? Of course you would—any writer would think my story was pathetic and laughable.'

'I'm not laughing at you, Adel. The people who told you that Leila Dahman died were telling the truth. And so were those who told you she's alive.'

'Please don't talk to me in riddles—I'm confused enough as it is, Walid.'

'Look, by accident I just found out that there's a Leila Dahman who's a neighbour of my cousin. I met her.'

'So Leila Dahman didn't die?'

'Meanwhile, in Jabalia Camp West, there's a woman—also a relative of ours—whose name is also Leila Dahman. She died of cancer just like they told you.'

He pauses, and looks at me quizzically.

'Look, I met the first Leila in person. She lives in Khan Yunis. She came with my cousin to greet me when I got here. When I asked my mother, she told me that the Leila who died of cancer was named Leila al-Sheikh Khalil Dahman. Her husband died shortly before she did—he was killed during a clash between Fatah and Hamas. The Leila who's alive is Leila al-Hajj Darwish Dahman. According to my mother, her husband is also dead—killed by a stray bullet.'

'That one is my Leila, Walid! The al-Hajj girl! That's right—people called her father al-Hajj, not al-Sheikh.

Can you tell me what she looks like?'

Adel seems more anxious now than he was when we first sat down. Maybe now that he can feel her so close, he also senses he might lose her for ever. As I begin to describe the attractive woman I met, his face begins to tremble, and his fingers tap nervously on the table. I tell him that even though the years have begun to erase some of her youth, she has held onto her beauty. She is tall, and full-figured. His fingers tap so hard that he nearly spills his coffee cup. I tell him that I did not get to speak to Leila, owing to her apparent shyness. I tell him that what I noticed most of all was how she talked. She liked to use the words, *and then*, as if they were a punctuation mark. 'Hmm, *and then* ...' 'She was, *and then* ...' 'Because, *and then* ...' If Leila could, she would stick the words between every two words she said.

Adel jumps up from his seat and throws his arms in the air, clenching his fists as if by doing so he could hold on to the moment for ever. He shouts, 'That's her! *And then* ... Adel, we're going to get married! Let the whole world be damned, *and then* ...! My Leila is alive, Walid!'

By now, Adel is jumping up and down, shouting: 'Leila's alive, Walid! Where have you been all my life?' Fortunately, there is no one else in the café besides us and the waiter, who is standing at the door, stifling the kind of laugh that would cost him a tip. Adel lifts me up and hugs me. In the commotion, he knocks over our cups and coffee and tea spill all over the tablecloth. The waiter rushes over, a black cloud hangs over him as he wipes up our mess.

Embarrassed, Adel says: 'I'm really sorry! I just heard the best news in the world. Give us a new tablecloth—if you want, I'll pay for this one. And the table too. I'll buy the whole restaurant if you want—anything to take that frown off your face.'

'Don't worry about it, sir,' the waiter says, by way of apology. 'We're here to serve our customers.'

Adel sticks his arm into his pocket and pulls out a hand whose fingers dance gingerly around a green fifty-dollar bill. He gives it to the waiter whose mouth hangs open so wide it looks like the nearby port of Gaza. 'This is for you. Keep the change.'

The waiter thanks Adel and walks off with much more than a week's pay in his pocket. At the waiter's suggestion, we move to another table that is clean, and he goes off to bring us fresh cups of coffee and tea, free of charge.

Adel cools down and savours the excitement. I begin to tell him that I will arrange a meeting for him with Leila's father, al-Hajj Darwish, if the man's still alive. If not, I can arrange for him to meet with another man from the family whose opinion matters as far as Leila is concerned, especially with regard to the question of marriage. It is a sensitive issue, especially given Leila's age. But Adel is adamant about marrying her—that is why he came to Gaza, after all. The only thing that remains in this long melodrama is the last episode—and

Adel will have to finish his story himself. I tell him that I hope it ends like any old Egyptian movie, with Leila standing barefoot on a windswept sand dune. Close-up on her face for a moment, then she flies down the sand calling out Adel's name. And there is Adel, dashing down the opposite dune, calling out her name. Close-up on the two lovers as they embrace. Fade out. The end.

Adel laughs. It seems as if a great burden has been lifted from him. He begins to run his fingers through his trim beard, and his eyes gleam like those of a groom on his wedding day. He turns to me and begins to recite the lines of poetry:

> I love Leila passionately, the way the soul loves, and Love is a seducer!
> O Exile of the heart, among the sons of the Dahman you will find her!
> And together, like old friends, we laugh our heads off.

15

In the afternoon, my cousin Abul-Abd proposes that we pray together. He leans hard into his right hand and then, clutching his cane in his left, rises to his feet. As he goes over to the mats spread out on the floor, he asks, 'Who's going to lead the prayers? Everybody? Come on, Abu Meshaal, would you? Abu Meshaal, could you come forward?'

Abu Meshaal stands up and the others in turn rise to pray behind him.

The man leading the other cousins in prayer right now is my father's cousin, whose full name is Samih Ismail Dahman. He is a midlevel Hamas organizer. Earlier, when he first walked into the room, people mentioned that he was preparing to nominate himself as one of the Hamas candidates for the Legislative Council elections. He earned his PhD. in economics from a university in the UK. Years ago, when he was in the final stages of writing his thesis, he sent me an email introducing himself. I was so happy to meet a cousin of mine, even though he had been born some time after I had gone away. It cheered me to know that there was another Dahman somewhere in Britain. His presence there somehow filled me with a feeling of real family. It was like having a glimpse of our country delivered to me. When he asked, I sent him a copy of my third novel. And despite being engrossed in his doctoral studies, he read it and let me know how much he admired it. When he asked me to send him a photo of my family, I did. When I asked him for a photo of his family, he did not hesitate. The person I saw in that picture was a young man in his early thirties. He had a long black beard and was going bald. There he stood, right between his young son and daughter. But that was all—the children's mother, or as we like to refer to mothers, *al-eila*, was absent, or absented. I did not need someone to explain it to me.

Abu Meshaal had sacrificed his better half to the new culture that was just beginning to conquer our society back then. Later, that culture would impose itself even more fiercely on the men in our family. In time, it even caught up with me. Samih's aunts, his father's sisters—Souad, Samira and Ibtisam—were beautiful young women, as delicate and lovely as tamarind flowers. Those girls used to hug me to death whenever I went to visit them in Shati Camp. Those girls—Samih's aunts—were my age, or thereabouts, and they went around with their hair uncovered, their arms and legs bare, sometimes wearing skirts that went above their knees. We were all of the same flesh, the same blood. I never felt anything in their hearts but their love and affection, and a fierce sense of pride about family. Back when I was a teenager, Abu Meshaal's aunts were my sisters and I was their brother.

And here I am at fifty-seven years of age, a British citizen now, with lots of experience of the world, and Abu Meshaal is hiding his wife from me and making sure I do not get a peek at her. And now this cousin of mine is leading everyone in prayer.

I was surprised by what I saw when he first walked in today. He was completely clean-shaven—no beard, no moustache. When I teased him about it, I told the whole room that in the UK, he had lived as a whiskered man among the beardless. He had been the Other. The Arab. The Muslim. He was Difference itself. But back in Gaza, he had no facial hair at all. Here he was—the image of the modern Muslim.

He laughs now and half turns to ask, 'Where are you, cousin? You back there behind me?'

'Behind you in every way, cousin!' I laugh back.

After receiving his first email, I decided not to coddle Abu Meshaal or delude him about myself. He and I began corresponding with one another. He would evangelize to me about the history of Islam, recounting its glorious past, and claiming, as so many others have, that when our society began to stray from religion, we fell into decay. He talked to me as if I knew nothing about Islam or history, as if he and his buddies were the first people to think up this revival stuff. As if it had never before been attempted. As if the Islamic state he talked about had not risen and fallen many times already, just like many other ancient and modern empires. I fought and pushed back until he was forced

207

to travel further and further back into a history he drew with a pen from times gone by, and with tired ideas that had been attempted so many times before. I pushed back until at last he stopped writing altogether. And when he disappeared, I did not hesitate for a moment to delete his photo from my computer.

I am the only man who remained seated when the others went to pray. An untouchable, like a seed planted in the wrong ground, I felt a strange kind of discomfort. Despite this, I did not want to be untrue to myself. I rejected the idea of presenting a false image, and did not want them to invent some persona for me, the way Abu Meshaal had once done with his outlandish beard. A character created to conform to the demands of time and place.

I begin to study everyone, and my mind forms a panorama of the Gaza I am visiting. Fresh sea breezes wrapped in the stench of open sewers. The wide sea hidden from view behind settlements. Women veiled in black, proclaiming to the world that they are forever in mourning, both for those who have passed away and also for those who have not yet done so. Currencies wrapped in shekels. A religion wrapped up in the notions of countless sheikhs. And a sun that struggles to rise from behind all these wrappings and veils, searching for a face to shine its light on—a sun which, ashamed by what it sees, then decides to hide itself again, tired and worn out by the effort of looking.

They finish praying, and I tell them that I hope their prayers have been heard. Some of them say goodbye and leave, others go back to where they were sitting and resume conversations, talk and arguments that might have been started a millennium ago and stories where the old and the new fold seamlessly into one another. Mahmoud Abbas becomes the caliph Harun al-Rashid, Yasser Arafat becomes Abu Dharr al-Ghifari, Abu Jaafar al-Mansour becomes Muhammad Dahlan, Mahmoud al-Zahar becomes Umar ibn al-Khattab, Ismail Haniya becomes Yasser Abed Rabbo.

It went on so long I began to imagine I was in an instant of time that was at war with another time, where different historical moments refused to admit this or that set of past events, and each rushed toward a final moment that would stop time for ever, or make it flow backwards.

16

On the drive to Khan Yunis, Abu Hatem points out Qarara and parks the old red Opel on the side of the road. I look out across the terrain, studying it, but not seeing where it is at all. There used to be a level crossing where cars had to pass over the railway line at the halfway point between Khan Yunis and Deir El-Balah—but now I cannot see it.

'Where are the tracks, Abu Hatem? A railway crossing is supposed to have train tracks, isn't it?'

'You still remember everything. The tracks are now about a hundred metres over there.' He points to the east. 'Behind the buildings on the other side.'

'Where did all the fig trees go?'

'They're still there—behind the buildings over there,' says Majdi who is sitting in the backseat. Majdi points to a set of tall buildings toward the west. The seven fig trees have always marked the Khan Yunis road. They were the first things that greeted you when you came from Deir El-Balah, and the last things you saw when you left Khan Yunis. These seven enormous trees had been planted decades ago, some said even centuries ago. And their small, bright-coloured fruit provided decent nourishment to those passing by.

Said the barber comes suddenly to mind. When we were twelve, we came out here one day by ourselves. We ate so many figs we were sick to our stomachs. After three intense, happy and all-consuming days with my mother, I have not had much time to think of old friends. But seeing these trees rekindles my memory.

'You know who these trees remind me of?'

'Who's that, Abu Fadi?'

My eyes continue to study the landscape, searching out those trees. 'My old childhood friend, Said Dahman.'

Neither says a word. After a while, the silence gets too heavy for me to bear, so I ask, 'What's wrong?'

'God rest his soul, cousin.'

'Said's dead?'

'He died three years ago, cousin. We thought you knew.'

I can barely breathe. The tears begin to well in my eyes, and I turn to look out of the window, wiping at my face with my sleeve. Thirty-eight years have gone by since I last saw this city, my second birthplace, and my childhood friends. And when I arrive at Khan Yunis, my best friend will not be there to welcome me.

'It'll be all right, Abu Fadi,' they tell me. From where he sits, Majdi pats my shoulder. Abu Hatem begins to tell me what happened, and I listen, quietly sobbing.

'You know how it is, no one expects something like that to happen. He was walking with his daughter-in-law and six-year-old grandson. The three of them were walking together, the boy in the middle, holding their hands and jumping around having fun. On that day, nothing was going on—everything was quiet. When they got to Ezzeddine al-Qassam School—remember it, Abu Fadi? It used to be a secondary school back in the day. When they got to the school, Said was struck in the chest by a bullet. It came from the observation post that overlooks our neighbourhood. The poor guy went down, and the woman started screaming and the boy— well, he just went berserk. Can you blame him? A little kid watching his grandfather as he died on the street. God help him and God help his mother for having to witness the event. People came running from all around. Someone called an ambulance—but to cut a long story short, by the time the paramedics got there, his time was up. God rest his soul, the poor man. Every Dahman and half the town came out for his funeral. Everybody loved that man. We loved how he laughed. We loved that man and we loved his stories.'

It was a real shock to hear Said was dead. It was the kind of loss that can never be recovered. He was a dear part of the past I had come here to collect. A major piece of my Khan Yunis childhood is taken away from me, just as I set foot here again.

It is almost 5 pm when we reach Jalal Street, the first avenue you get to if you are coming from the north. The first evening breezes waft through the windows. Abu Hatem recites the name of every street we pass. The only memories I have of these places are their names—I have forgotten what the places themselves looked like. Around us, buildings clamber over one another on both sides of the street. And people. Crowds of people of all ages, walking every which way down each and every street.

We arrive in El-Amal, my cousin's neighbourhood. It is no more than a pile of debris fallen from the sky and called 'buildings'—just as the piles of Jabalia and Beit Lahia once fell and grew. El-Amal sits on a strip of fine yellow sand dunes that stretch parallel to the agricultural strip from Rafah City to the outskirts of Deir El-Belah. El-Amal separates the agricultural land from the sea, except for the small spur of irrigated farmland known as al-Muwasi, that juts out to the west of Khan Yunis. The entire area behind the camp had been forested with shady acacia trees so as to prevent the sand from stealing into Khan Yunis.

Nowadays, the thing that steals over the city is the strip of settlements known as the Qatif Bloc. These colonies have effectively confiscated not only Khan Yunis' lands, but its sea as well. When we were young, we used to play on these little hills—and it seemed as if the azure horizon was what made our eyes sparkle with joy.

The next day, late in the morning, Abu Hatem asks me whether I slept well. He had already asked me that question earlier in the morning, just before he went off to the garment factory he owned. We were sitting on the ground floor of the apartment building he built with the sweat of years of hard work. Then, in the afternoon, he asks me again what I did with myself all day. I tell him I spent my morning wandering around town, trying to get a feel for what it has become. I tell him that the Khan Yunis I knew no longer exists. I had searched out the khanyunisian essence of the place everywhere, but never found it, for the remnants of the old place were buried beneath the surfaces of the contemporary city. As I walked around the main streets, I often felt like I knew it, even though there was nothing tangible that would lead me to believe this. There was no trace of the streetlamp in whose glow I used to bask all night. The shop where I bought cigarettes is now gone, along with the café where I used to play cards with friends. Even the dirt courtyard where I used to walk barefoot is gone. Beneath the surface of the place, other buried impressions take form here and there. It is like looking at a black and white photograph whose details are blurred by the passing of years.

On trembling legs, I stop and stare at the strange patch of exile where my home once stood. There are no traces left, of it or of my childhood. Not even of the shadow I used to chase and chase and sometimes even catch. My shadow and I were careful never to let each other stray too far, and so our game never ended, and our friendship was never broken. I have left no footprint here to find. The cement beneath my feet chokes whatever memory lies below, just as it does the air I once exhaled here so long ago—breath whose traces still seek to find me once more.

I wander through streets that swallow people who crowd into cars and donkey-drawn carts. The streets swallow the jeeps of the militias and the armoured cars stuffed with men who watch the pedestrians through small holes in black hoods. I feel truly alone here—of no significance to anyone, nor is there anyone here who means anything to me. I come upon the spot where Café Mansour once stood. The biggest of all the city's coffee shops, and the nicest one on the city's main square. I find only small commercial shops teeming with shoppers. I can see my father, sitting right there on a bamboo chair next to his table. There is his cup of hot tea, sprigs of mint sticking out. There is the steam rising into the air with its sweet minty smell. I can hear the men nearby as they slap down dominoes on the marble tabletops around me. I love the way that tapping and clacking rings in my ears. Somewhere here, forty-five years ago, my father sat and was suddenly struck down.

Just as the years have changed me, so too am I transformed by the sudden recollection of my father and his death. I decide to visit his grave. I have always hated visiting cemeteries, but now I am struck by the urge to do it. When I lived here, I visited my father's grave only twice, once to inspect the gravestone, and once again—just before my departure—because my mother told me to.

When I get to the graveyard, I find that there is no longer any gate to speak of. I continue along toward my father's grave. The only things I find are piles of rocks and the fragments of headstones. I turn them upside down searching for my father's name, but find nothing. Not even a letter that might belong in his name.

A bitter despair washes over me as I stand there. I think about how my father's spirit haunts this place—and it feels like I am the one responsible for losing my father's remains. I turn and spy the desiccated stump of a tree—maybe that was the acacia that stood over my father's grave for all those years. The tree in whose branches fluttered those rose-embroidered silk handkerchiefs that proclaimed the undying love of someone for someone else. Those have all disappeared into nothing, never divulging who was speaking to whom.

The stump rekindles an old question in my mind. *Who was it that hung the handkerchiefs in the branches?*

Abu Hatem asks me: 'Where did you go after that?' I tell him that I continued walking to the old seed market and found the place exactly how it used to be. The joy I feel at this discovery more than makes up for the grief I experienced at the graveyard. When I wander over to the Ironsmiths' Market nearby, I am even happier. The Ottoman-era shops still have the same age-old appearance, even if they are all shuttered and covered with rust-eaten locks. Only now do I begin to believe I am truly back in Khan Yunis.

Guided by the old map of my memory, I continue along. Within a few minutes, I find myself in front of the old Hurriyya Summer Movie House. Said Dahman is standing to my right, and Fawzi Ashour to my left. The three of us are staring up, gawking at a huge poster hanging on the façade of the cinema. It is a larger-than-life image of the Egyptian belly dancer, La Petite Nawal. We study the more obvious contours of her body, in hopes we might discover subtleties hidden within. Each of us hoping that a breeze would lift up and play with the patch of chiffon flitting between her thighs.

One of the bouncers yells and pushes us away. 'If you don't have a ticket, you're not coming in. Step back if you don't have a ticket already.'

A bunch of kids crowds round the door, shouting and yelling—and so we join them, pushing and trying to rush through. But the door is blocked by two bouncers with bodies like bulldozers.

Gradually, we give way and retreat—until we end up back down the stairs and out on the public pavement. After about thirty minutes, everyone who has bought a ticket is already inside.

At this point, Said—who is the bravest of us—goes up to one bouncer stationed outside the door. 'You happy about all this?' he asks as a joke. 'These kids are the future of our nation, and they don't get to watch simply because they have no money?'

The bouncer smiles. 'You kids are too young. And you're twerps to boot. But I'm going to let you in anyway. One by one, so nobody notices. Don't let the manager see you, he's standing inside.' He points to a man whose watermelon body sits near the entrance.

'Get ready. After the trailers finish, I'll let you in.'

The man opens the door, and we sneak in one by one just as he told us to. We are lucky—for some reason the manager has left. Maybe the ticket receipts of the paying customers were more than enough to make him happy.

We go over to the side, sticking close to one another, against the wall. Nawal is shaking her arse and twisting this way and bending over that way, like she was teasing all of us—this room full of men who were not only powerless to resist the allure of her body, but had even purchased tickets to feel that sense of powerlessness. And then, as Nawal shimmies around, there is Farid El-Atrache, crooning away.

> *He said nothing to me*
> *And I said nothing to him*
> *He didn't come looking for me,*
> *And I didn't go looking for him.*

And as the long-simmering desire of the men in the audience begins to fizzle out, they begin to chirp and call, moan and clap, and finally they are whistling their appreciation. These are men who have never before seen live flesh on stage, and may never see it in their dreams either, even if their wives sleep right next to them in bed each night.

Nawal dances on and on, the chiffon patch between her legs flitting up and away now and then to reveal what it conceals beneath. And the three of us try our best to take it all in with six bulging eyes. Fawzi is swooning over Farid El-Atrache, and keeps yelling: 'Farid, you're the best! Abdel Halim can go to hell!' He goes on and on like this so long that Said finally belts him in the back of the neck, yelling, 'What's with you, you idiot? What's the deal with Abdel Halim anyway? Can't you just shut up and watch the movie?' So Fawzi starts up again, only this time without insulting Abdel Halim. Then an older kid, standing right next to Fawzi, starts up, kicking Fawzi hard until finally he shuts up.

A tall boy climbs up on stage at one point and begins to dance and shake his body around. When he throws his arms over Nawal's body, the whole place erupts in loud protest—that is how badly they want to do the very thing he is doing. The three of us go crazy too, it is the first time in our lives we have ever seen bare legs.

That night, I cannot sleep. I am walking through a forest of bare legs. I am pretty sure that Said and Fawzi also spent their night walking through the same fleshy landscape. I suspect that, like me, neither of them slept until their underwear was drenched.

I stand at the corner of the cinema, looking at the building. On the wall, I read a notice put up by the Organization of Women of Virtue. *One era has come to take the place of another in this country. Each moment in time attempts to erase the one that came before—and when it does, it brings a curse down on all.*

'That's pretty much what I saw in Khan Yunis, Abu Hatem.'

But my answer does not fully satisfy Abu Hatem. He asks, 'Was anything in Khan Yunis like how you remembered it?'

'Cousin, I never found the Khan Yunis I came looking for.'

I wake up at dawn on Friday. The silver sky quickly surrenders to a warm sun making ready for a beautiful day. In our last telephone conversation, two days before I left London, Abu Hatem had insisted he would host a feast on my behalf when I came. When I saw him in the last bachelor pad on my first night in Jabalia, he had renewed that pledge—and now Abu Hatem is doing everything he needs to do to get ready for the day.

Immediately after noon prayers, men—young and old—from all sides of the family begin to pour in. Platters of meat and rice are laid out and another scene begins to unfold, borne in on a warm sense of family. More than one hundred men of all ages are gathered together, devouring the food before them and exchanging greetings and questions with me. Some I am meeting for the first time. Others are old friendships rekindled as we sit in the tent they have erected for the occasion on the rooftop.

Suddenly, I cannot get the thought of Muhammad Samoura out of my head. Will he be happy to see me? Will Muhammad recognize himself in the image of the tailor he is in my memory? Muhammad has been a police officer for a very long time now. In his life as a tailor, he never managed to put enough order into a pair of trousers to make their seat fit their wearer's arse. And now, as a police colonel, he is in charge of law and order. Most cops are Fatah supporters. Even if he was not one before, he had to become one. Will you dare ask him about all the corruption, knowing that he is one of those whose job it is to protect the corrupt? He will just shake his head and tell you it is a matter of state security. If you ask him about all the thieves, he will probably tell you that the PA is on the job—even though you both know that it was the PA who brought the real thieves with them when they arrived.

Still, I love Muhammad and badly want to see him. He will not believe it when he sees me—he will probably joke: 'Walid! I'm going to have to detain you all summer so we can really visit with you!'

I take Abu Hatem aside. When Majdi sees us, he hurries over to join us.

'Where's Col. Muhammad, Abu Hatem?'

He does not answer. Then he asks, 'You mean Muhammad Samoura?'

'I want to see at least one of my old friends while I'm here!'

Abu Hatem does not say anything. The same look of consternation that I saw yesterday when I asked about Said now appears on his face. When he begins to shake his head, the same fear begins to jab at my heart.

'What is it? Why aren't you speaking, Abu Hatem? I want to see Muhammad. You invited him, didn't you?'

'How could I, cousin? Look, no offence, but you don't live here and you don't understand what's going on. There's bad blood between us and the Samouras. One of them killed one of us.'

Majdi jumps in to explain. 'Your friend has a cousin who's in the National Security Forces. He got into some ugly words with another officer he worked with, Fuad Dahman. Even though they were good friends and worked together, they quarrelled and fought until it got really bad. One day the Samoura kid pulled out his pistol and shot Fuad. No one in the family was willing to take the blood money or make up with them. No one wants to let go of what happened—and no one has forgotten it. You know how it is—blood is thicker than water, cousin.'

Our family now kills and is killed. What kind of family is this that I've come back to?

'Abu Fadi, would you have wanted me to invite your friend and throw him to the Dahmans? He wouldn't have come had I invited him.'

At this moment, I finally grasp that I live in a world separate from theirs, and that Gaza has gone backwards fifty years in time. It is senseless to continue opening up old files.

Abu Hatem agrees to let the matter drop while I try to digest this news, the second shock I have felt since my arrival.

17

On another night in Khan Yunis, another guest descends upon us. Who it was that beckoned him, I do not know. It may well have been Abu Faruq, who was introduced to me on the night of the feast. The man who would not stop telling everybody that he was Abu Hatem's pharmacist friend. It was probably him, but it could have been any one of the thirty or so relatives who had come to spend the evening with us. In any case, I did hear someone beckon the illustrious guest, even if he did not actually mention the man by name. All he had to do was say 'the pride of the Arabs' and everyone knew who he was talking about.

Saddam Hussein? Now it's getting good, I tell myself as I switch on the tiny digital recorder I have been carrying in my shirt pocket. The only part of the device that shows is a gold clip that looks like it's part of an expensive pen. The words are still in my mouth when a voice booms out from the middle of the room. 'Nothing has fucked us up like that buddy of yours, Abu Faruq.'

So it was the pharmacist who said it? I turn to see how Abu Faruq is going to respond to the challenge.

'He is, despite what you and others might say, the best of the best. A real Arab.' Abu Faruq's voice rises above the bubbling of the shisha and the murmuring of the men. And then he throws the ball in my lap. 'What do you think, Abu Fadi? You're a journalist. You know better than us.'

I exhale, the thick smoke rises into the air. I take cover in a non-committal answer. 'I didn't come to talk, Abu Faruq. I came to listen.' I let my recorder run, taping the evening's conversation.

'Abu Faruq, what's so brave about hiding an old missile or two, and then firing them on Israel and sending everyone in the region to hell, Iraq included?'

'Shakir, who was the one who helped you at the start of the Intifada?'

'You mean: who was paying people to carry his photo around on placards? Who was ruining our reputation throughout the whole world? Fifty dollars for anyone hit by a rubber bullet. One hundred dollars for a real bullet. Two to four thousand for your family if you die. It doesn't matter if you're injured or killed— all that matters is that someone gets hit. The money's there, waiting to be spent. Then, one day the money's all gone and all we're left with are our dead and crippled. Gaza's full of them. How did this help our cause?'

'OK, let's not get too hung up about Saddam and his bombs. Listen, I want to tell you about what happened to me one night when I was coming back from Tel Aviv.'

'Don't try to change the subject, Abu Hatem.'

'Majdi, *habibi*, listen. We talk about the Saddam phenomenon all the time, let me tell my story and you'll see. Abu Fadi, this really happened to me during the First Intifada. I got to Beit Hanoun crossing at about 1 in the morning. Luckily for me, the soldier on duty was this gorgeous Indian girl. She looked just like the actress in that film *Singam*, way back when there used to be cinemas in Gaza. God have mercy on us these days! Remember when Gazans could play hooky by going to the movies? Where was I? The Jewish girl. The Indian girl. Right when she puts the magnetic strip of my ID card into the computer, the screen goes dead. I say to myself: *That's it, the central computer's down, I'm going to have to spend the night here.* The girl asks me: "Do you have a permit?" I say: "I swear. It's in my ID." But she doesn't understand what I'm saying, so I tell her to call the officer in charge. He comes over, stretching and yawning. "Where you coming from, *khabibi*?" he says. I tell him I'm coming from a friend's wedding in Tel Aviv. He starts typing and says: "Wait here." Then he sees something that tells him I'm good to go. I let him mess around with his computer and decide to call Mr Sha'ul, the guy whose house I was at. At first he is bent out of shape because I'm calling him so late. Then he asks: "*Efo ata*, Abu Khatem? What's going on? Where are you?" I tell him I'm at the crossing and that they're not letting me through. He says: "Put the officer on the phone." I give the phone to the officer and they start talking. Next thing you know, these guys are laughing their heads off and chatting away. After about five minutes, he tells the Indian girl: "Let him through." The point is, everyone, Mr. Sha'ul and I were like friends. Even closer. We worked together for fifteen years or so. We worked together throughout the First Intifada. Throughout the founding of the PA. And then things got bad. One time we were even thrown into jail together. OK, we weren't incarcerated, but we were detained. The army tried to hold us for taxes we paid or didn't pay. The point is: we suffered and succeeded together. He used to come visit me in Rafah when the garment factory was there. He came to see me in Khan Yunis when it was too dangerous for me to go to him. What I mean is this: we had a real relationship. A friendship through thick and thin. He must be seventy by now. Could I have another coal for my arghileh, Abul-Nun?'

Everybody calls Abu Hatem's son, Nabil, 'Abul-Nun'. Nabil comes over, carrying hot coals in a metal colander, and puts some on each arghileh.

Hassan Dahman works in a garment factory in one of the settlements close to Khan Yunis. Now he picks up the thread of the conversation and begins to embroider on the subject of bilateral relations. 'Back during the First Intifada, cousin, the Jews used to come to visit us. They used to come to our weddings and bring their children with them. They'd come to congratulate the bride and groom. They'd come to the wedding and dance with us. None of us had any problems with anything.'

'Yeah, it's the Second Intifada that ruined everything. All the dying, the shooting and suicide bombs. That's what blew up everything we had, Hassan.'

'That's right. If only the Intifadas hadn't happened. If only we'd stuck to the old slogan of a secular, democratic state—the two peoples would have been assimilated into one another by now. You know, a lot of Palestinians married Jewish girls and got citizenship.'

'You're dreaming, Abu Hatem! Your mind is all mixed up by Uncle Sha'ul and all the business you do.'

'You're mistaken, Abu Jalal. The First Intifada revived the Israeli left and made it stronger.'

'So the First Intifada fixed all our problems? I beg to differ. The Intifada is what fucked us up good. The First Intifada brought us Oslo, right? And Oslo brought us the PA, right? Go look outside and see all the thuggery and corruption the PA brought to the country. Then it fucked itself up and left us with nothing but occupation.'

'The First Intifada was a popular insurrection. Everyone got involved. Even dogs took part in the struggle. Who else remembers what Abu Khaled's dog did during the First Intifada?'

When no one answers, he goes on. 'Apparently I'm the only one who knows it. I heard the story from folks in Breij Camp.'

'Tell us the story then, Jumaa,' someone finally calls out. Others chime in, inviting him to go on.

'One day, the chief Israeli commander is touring Breij Camp in his jeep. The jeep stops and he gets out of the vehicle. Back in the day, Abu Khaled El-Jirjani had a dog called Bobby. Bobby sees the officer and begins to bark at him. When the kids in the neighbourhood notice, they start cheering Bobby on, clapping and whistling: "Bite him, Bobby! Eat him up, chew his bones!" The dog gets riled up even more and begins to bark louder and louder. The next thing you know, Bobby's flying through the air. He's like a panther pouncing on the officer, locking his jaws on the man. At first the Israeli is completely stunned, then he manages to grab his gun and he shoots Bobby. Then he jumps into his jeep and takes off as fast as he can, while the poor dog lies dying in a pool of his own blood. Those kids went and picked up Bobby's body. I swear to you, those kids picked up that dog and put him on their shoulders like they were carrying the body of a soldier who'd been killed on the battlefield. Of course, the Jews couldn't do anything to stop them from doing it. Those kids went around saying that Bobby was a true patriotic hero. They were crying, with real tears in their eyes, and singing.

By our souls, by our blood,
We will ransom you, O Bobby!

To cut a long story short, people, they dug a grave for the dog and buried him. He was the first dog martyr of the cause.'

'I've heard that story before, Jumaa. I don't want to ruin it for you. But the truth of it is that he wasn't any braver or more patriotic than other dogs. He just knew that the Jew wasn't from the camp and didn't belong.

That's all. Then he attacked. I remember the dog. I was pretty broken up about it when he died.'

'God have mercy on that dog's soul. What do you think, Abu Fadi, do you think Israel's ever going to pull out of Gaza?'

'Yes, Abu Faruq. It wants to leave. Sharon's as sick and tired of Gaza as everyone else who came before. He wants to get rid of Gaza—not because he gives a damn about the people who live here, but so that he can hold all the keys himself and slam the door shut whenever he wants to.'

'Damned if they occupy us and damned if they pull out!'

Suddenly, I start thinking about Salim Abu Shanab, a journalist I met in Tunis years ago. And I remember a story he told me when I visited him three days ago at the press office he works at. We had been talking about the current situation, analysing it from so many angles that it began to dissolve on our tongues. I asked him whether he agreed that a kind of tribalism—or clannishness—had returned to Gaza after so many years. I asked whether he agreed that this mindset had crept into everyone's heads now, including intellectuals' who should know better. He leaned back in his chair, took a long drag of his cigarette, then answered, 'Listen, my friend. It's easy to explain. If no one's got your back, you're dead. Look at me, I write all the time in a lot of papers. I appear on television. I have personally gone after the PA. I have been critical of Hamas as well—but no one can touch me.

And that's because before anyone is going to come after you, they're going to size you up. Who are you? Who are you related to? Who's got your back? How strong is your family? Are you with the PA? And so on. Listen, let me tell you a story that will explain how it works. There was a Hamas preacher called Abul-Sibhat, because of all the prayer beads he played with. The guy attacked me all the time. Every Friday, this guy had nothing better to do than abuse me. During his sermon, he'd go on and on about this heretical apostate journalist Abu Muhannad, meaning yours truly. One Friday, my cousin Bassam—he's a really good guy, you'd like him—was praying in Abul-Subuhat's mosque. Bassam listened to the man attack me like he did every week. The microphone was turned up so loud you could hear it all the way to the outskirts of Rafah Camp. Bassam waited after prayers and then went up to the guy. He says: "God bless you, sheikh." The guy must have thought Bassam had come to thank him for the great sermon, so he replies: "God bless you too. Welcome, dear brother." So my cousin says, "Do you know who that heretic Salim Abu Shanab is?" Abul-Subuhat strokes his beard from top to bottom and gently answers: "Let's not talk about that apostate. May the curses of God be upon him!" "Listen up, you old coot," my cousin shouts. Then Bassam starts yelling at the sheikh while sparks shoot out of his eyes, "That man—the one you say is an apostate—he's my cousin. He's part of my family. We're the Abu Shanabs—don't forget the name. If you ever utter anything negative about him, I'm going to rip your beard out. Even if you surround yourself with twenty other old sheikhs and a hundred militiamen, I'll come in here and break your knees."

'"Salim Abu Shanab's your cousin?" the sheikh asks, squirming like a cockroach in a drain. Of course, he never expected that someone would speak to him like that. Our pious brother had built his entire reputation on abusing me. He put on a caliph's cloak and built a small kingdom for himself in a mosque while gathering followers around him. And every Friday, they'd entertain themselves cursing the Satan of the Press as they used to call me. The devil of the secular apostates. And now along comes someone who doesn't only hold him accountable for what he says, but chastises him for it too. Our sheikh friend starts to tremble. As he tries to justify himself, his beard sweeps back and forth on the ground like a soft broom, "Did I say something wrong?" My cousin Bassam reminds him of all the punishments he is going to suffer if he doesn't quit. The old man is shaking and stuttering as he utters the most earnest of oaths: "I swear to God, I swear to God, if I'd known Salim was your cousin, I would have kept my thoughts about him to myself." "I don't want you to speak about him. I don't want you to have any thoughts about him either. Do you hear me, old man? Or do you want me to bury you upside down in the sand?"

'You know what happened after that? Every time that sheikh saw my cousin, he'd ask: "How's Salim, I mean, Abu Muhannad? Please send him my best wishes and kindest regards."'

The memory of this conversation makes me suddenly laugh out loud. Abu Hatem turns to me and asks, 'What's so funny, Abu Fadi? You don't like the conversation?'

'Not at all. Everyone's entitled to their own opinion, cousin.'

When the party shuts down, I turn the recorder off. There is enough dialogue here to fill ten pages.

18

Abu Hatem takes me on a tour of Gaza City so I can see my friend Muhammad Khadija. On the way there, I cannot stop thinking about Adel El-Bashity. I thought I was done with it. I thought I had handed the keys back to their owner. But as soon as I thought about it again, I began to realize I was mistaken. There were so many unanswered questions. Had the keys to Leila's heart rusted after all these years? Or might they still open that door? Or would she keep away from the whole thing, given how scandalous a reunion might be? Or would it be he who backed off when he finally began to face the absurdity of those feelings he'd carried around for so many years?

All of a sudden Adel seemed cheap to me. He had used me at our meeting. I had handed him the keys that would unlock an old, neglected room in his heart. I had paved the way for him to enjoy the remainder of his days. And up till now, Adel had not even called to thank me. By now, he has met his Leila. He must have. If he had not, my mobile would be ringing the whole time, with him asking me to resume the search for Leila. It is just like the Palestinian–Israeli negotiations—they are always resumed one way or another. Sometimes they go forward, sometimes they falter, but even then, they're resumed, and we all breathe a sigh of relief to know they have not yet died. And then they stumble again.

Why get upset about Adel El-Bashity? Don't we say, *Saw his girl, forgot the world*? And besides, we were not even friends to begin with. We had only met because he was searching for Leila. That is the extent of it.

The fact is I liked Adel El-Bashity more in my novel than I did in real life. The fictional character was more authentic. And besides, what do you hope for from authenticity when the character departs from the text and begins to get mixed up with the real Adel? Isn't that what happened when the three of us sat there in the Andalus Hotel Café, talking about Leila? Didn't Adel find his two beings at that moment? Didn't the two versions join together at that moment to rebel against me, the author?

I do not like the idea that this is how my protagonist will end up. I miss the Adel El-Bashity whose footsteps I was following, through light and shadow, fact and fiction, until I got to where I am.

Abu Hatem parks the car next to the curb, gets out and starts walking. I run to catch up to him. In my hand, I am holding the small statue of Nefertiti I have been carrying with me for so long.

Abu Hatem points to a man squatting on the ground. He is hunched over himself, leaning against the walls of the Tel al-Zuhur Hospital. Next to him is a long cane.

Reluctantly, I begin to approach. My heart is trembling. When, at last, I am standing directly over him, I begin to look hard at what is left of the man who, long ago, was my best friend. Now he is this beggar whose right hand hangs in the air for hours at a time, snatching whatever drops from the hands of people walking by. *I brought you Nefertiti, Muhammad. Remember how you knew how to sculpt her in the air? That image has remained on display in my mind ever since. Who turned your artist's hand into a purse for shekels? Who made you sit there, asking for handouts, an object of scorn and pity?*

I think I am going to leave. I shut my eyes, unable to keep looking at the shape Muhammad is in. This is an unrecognizably distorted copy of the boy whose friendship had lit up my childhood. Abu Hatem waits for me a short way off. I turn away so no one can see the tears in my eyes.

Instead of walking off, I suddenly say hello. Muhammad answers me warmly. I reach into my pocket and take out two hundred dollar bills. As I put them into Muhammad's palm, his fingers curl around the bills until they are swallowed in a tight fist. I press his hand to his chest and say: 'That's two hundred dollars, my deserving friend. I hope to give you fifty more each month ...'

But he interrupts me before I can finish. 'Look here, brother. I'm an old man, so please don't tease me. May God ease your days.'

'I'm not joking, brother. It really is two hundred dollars. Hold them in your hand.'

He lifts his head, bends first to the right, then again to the left. Exactly like he used to do when he wanted to figure out who it was who was talking to him. Then he laughs out loud. 'God bless—and hear your prayers, brother! Is there anyone who gives anyone two hundred dollars these days? Even sons and brothers don't do that for each other! Look, let's leave it at one hundred. That's more than enough. Or would you rather give me one hundred in shekels? Take your money and go your way, my good man.'

His fingers are now carefully inspecting the bills, even as he tries to hand them back to me. 'It's a good deed you're trying to do for this poor old man. May God reward you for it!'

'Muhammad, I'm not playing a trick on you. That is two hundred dollars you have in your hands.'

'So you also know my name?'

'Of course I do, you're Muhammad Rayan.'

His left hand gropes across the ground searching for his cane, while the money still hangs in the fingers of his other hand. He leans over to stand up, and by now it is clear that I have rattled him. I reach out and touch his shoulder, urging him not to get up. He sits back down, and says aloud: 'No one in Gaza City knows Muhammad Rayan. Muhammad Rayan disappeared long ago. You're looking at Abu Saber, the most famous beggar in the entire Gaza Strip. Ask anyone from Beit

Hanoun all the way to Rafah—they'll know where to find me. Ask anyone at any of the Israeli checkpoints—they'll all tell you that you can always find me sitting at City Hall. Is Israel shelling Gaza today? Is Fatah clashing with Hamas, or just with itself? Is there a family feud raging somewhere? It doesn't matter—Abu Saber is sitting in his usual spot at City Hall. And he'll go on sitting there until someone decides it's time for him to close up his begging shop.'

'But City Hall used to be Tel al-Zuhur Hospital, didn't it, Muhammad Khadija?'

'Who are you? You're not from here. Everyone who used to know me by that name is long gone.'

I wish I could put Nefertiti in his hands and let his fingers feel it. Let his fingers feel it all over and remind him of the image he once drew for us. But I worry how it might affect him.

I step away and decide to leave Muhammad to his hazy misgivings. Sometimes doubts are better than the truth—they allow us to turn them over in our minds for a while until, bored, we are happy to return to our old selves.

I grab both of his hands and shake them, saying goodbye as I turn. 'Farewell, Muhammad, my friend. You'll get your fifty dollars on the first of each month. Please, please stop begging and go back to who you were before, Muhammad Khadija. As soon as you do that, someone will come to tell you who I am.'

Nefertiti rests in my hands as I walk away. Abu Hatem has already got into the car and is sitting behind the steering wheel. Before opening the door and getting in, I turn around and see Muhammad standing there, leaning on his cane.

Abu Hatem turns the key in the ignition and Muhammad realizes I am about to go. He waves his cane around in the air and screams so loudly it splits my heart. As we drive away, he calls out: 'Who are you—you stranger who is not a stranger?'

I stick my arm out of the window and let the breeze catch and tug it up and down. When we get to the top of Tel al-Zuhur hill, I fling the statuette as far as I can. I imagine Nefertiti sliding and tumbling down the hill, all the way to Firas market at the very bottom.

'Why didn't you tell Abu Saber who you were?' asks Abu Hatem. 'You broke his heart—and mine too.'

'I couldn't do it. It would have been worse had he known it was me. If he knew I saw him like that.'

Abu Hatem turns to look at me. 'There's only one other friend left, Walid.' He speaks the words as if saying them were a relief. 'Muhammad al-Misriyya. Before you ask, I'm going to tell you everything up front. I haven't seen him or heard anything about him for twenty years. The world has gone to hell and nobody is who they used to be. Everybody I know lost their head a long time ago—and everybody's still looking for where they put it.'

The car drives us out of Gaza and down the road back to Jabalia.

19

Abu Hatem, his wife Amina and their two sons Nasser and Salim are the last people to say goodbye. When they walk out of the apartment, they gather up their sadness and tears and carry it away with them. I remain there for long minutes, my eyes following them as they descend the stairs, watching their hands creep down the banister floor by floor. I listen to the sound of their footsteps growing more and more distant, then those too fade away. At last, the closing of the front door announces that the moment of goodbyes has come to an end. And, as the latch clicks shut, a moment of my life also closes. When that door opens again in the morning, it will be to announce my departure, and the beginning of what is to come.

Now, there are only a few of us left in the apartment—besides my mother and me, there is Amal, Emad, Nasreen, their daughter, and Nasr, their younger son. Shafiq is also there, the last bachelor, who tonight announces that he has decided to get divorced from bachelorhood as soon as he can. My mother almost lets out a piercing ululation, but covers her mouth before anything comes out. The death of his brother Falah is still recent, and the rules of mourning still cast their shadow over any wedding celebration.

I wish Shafiq a happy marriage and tell him that his apartment will not relish the prospect of being renamed. He proposes a new nickname—the new groom's pad—and adds: 'It might help spawn a birth and then I might become an Abu So-and-So!'

Throughout the days I have spent in Jabalia, Amal has been tireless in preparing our meals and taking care of everything. She is like our second, younger mother. She sits opposite me now, watching me intensely, as if she sees right through me. The whole time, she is collecting moving, living images of me to keep in her mind's album. Emad sits there without speaking, looking back and forth at my mother and me. My mother's tongue has finally stopped moving, and not because of any device. Now it is she who needs someone who will comfort her on the eve of her son's departure.

I look at Nasreen—she usually gabs as much as a talk-show guest and if anyone ever needed a remote device under her tongue, it is she. But tonight, I am astonished that she too has nothing to say.

It is almost 10 pm. Each of us has settled into silence. Each of us thinks about what to say, then decides there is nothing more to be said. I am worried, thinking about Abu Hatem. By now, they have covered most of the distance on their way home to Khan Yunis. I am bothered by the fact that on their way they have to pass through the Israeli checkpoint at Mahfouza, which cuts the Strip right in half. As if I was not already worried enough about what I will encounter tomorrow.

This is my last night in the Gaza Strip. My trip has lasted twenty-one days. I have gathered impressions and stories like shadows for an album of ghost images. I have let Adel El-Bashity go wherever he wants with Leila Dahman, after supplying him with enough family to keep him safe and enough detail to make it all plausible.

I will let the other characters in my novel fend for themselves. I will let each of them rebel against me as they like. I will let each of them create their own plot for the coming days, and I will not interfere at all as narrator. From now on, the characters will be in charge of their own plausibility.

Somewhere, nearby, there is a huge explosion that shakes the floor we are sitting on. Then we hear helicopters, chopping by at a distance, and short blasts of gunfire. I jump up and stand at the window to see what is happening.

'Get down!' My mother screams until I am sitting by her side again. 'I don't want you to get hit. Tomorrow you're going back to your family, and we want you to get there safely.'

I sit squatting on the floor, feeling upset and despondent. I have grown used to sitting this way, but my buttocks are looking forward to touching a real chair again. Any chair—even a cushionless plastic one like those we sat on at Abu Hatem's on the day of the feast. My mother is worried about stray bullets. No wonder. After twenty days here, I have learned to cultivate a healthy fear of stray bullets, and the cheap, unannounced death they bring. Said Dahman was killed by a stray bullet. Leila Dahman's first husband died the same way, as did the husband of the other Leila Dahman. It is as if Gazans live in a permanent condition of randomness. Death wanders about as a stray, and each time it chooses its victim, it does so at random. There is the kind of death that is predictable and planned, and those who want that kind of end know how to find it. There is the unpredictable kind of death that happens according to the shifting balance of power between the various militias. There is also natural death, its victims necessarily in the dark about when it will arrive. And then there is the gratuitous, absurd kind of death whose hand falls according to no plan or pattern. One and a half million Palestinians crowded together, living in the most unpredictable way this unpredictable form of life, living for a death that comes and goes. I now understand why, when you are here, it's impossible to catch a glimpse of the world outside. Now I understand why no one talks about 'happiness' or 'the future'. Only the last bachelor does, as he plans a wedding in this mass graveyard, in the hopes that he might father many children who will join him in waiting for a future that is always only murky.

Another explosion crashes outside, and Abdelfettah rushes in, clutching a transistor radio that broadcasts non-stop chatter. He tells us he has been listening to Sawt al-Hurriyya station. We gather around him and listen, heads down, trembling.

In addition, two Qassam rockets ... Our corre-
spondent in Gaza now joins us to give us more details
about the incident ...

Al-Salaamu 'aleikum, brother Ayman, could you tell
us what you know about the latest developments in the
story?

Brother Namiq ...

The voice disappears. Then, moments later, it comes
back.

... ibed. Zionist occupation force ...

Now Nasreen is arguing with her brother, Nasr.

There are tan ... the occup ...

'Will you two shut up?!' Emad screams. 'We're
trying to ... Now, get your backsides in bed!' Emad
turns to his wife. 'Could you go get the other radio,
Amal? Abdelfettah's isn't working very well.'

As Abdelfettah jiggles the dial, hoping for better re-
ception, Amal runs upstairs.

That's in addition to the two missiles that hit the
settlement. There's a great deal of activity inside the
compound, as well as unusual military movements
on the part of occupation forces in the... Occupation
aircraft have resumed ... Beit Hanoun, and in the
vicinity of the hospital.

Will the bombardment let up before tomorrow
morning? Will the crossing be closed because of this?
These missiles are a disaster—there is no possible up-
side to the stupid attack now taking place.

The planes have just renewed their attacks, but we're

not yet able to ascertain their exact target.

Amal returns with another radio and hands it to Emad who starts spinning through the stations.

It seems we've lost our connection to Brother Ayman ...

Abdelfettah turns his off.

Oh, oh, oh! How I miss your beautiful eyes!
Oh, oh, oh! How scared I am for you!
Oh, oh, oh!

'This radio has no shame!' My mother is incensed. 'Is this any time to be playing songs about my eyes and your eyes? I hope the monkey who gave birth to them rips out their eyes!'

'I've got a way to play al-Manar on my mobile,' Abdelfettah remarks. 'I want to listen to that.'

In Beit Hanoun, at the hospital, Namiq.

Please go ahead, Brother Ayman. Please continue.

Yes, Namiq. There are attacks on Beit Lahia in the north. Six ...

Emad tries tuning into other stations until he loses patience, then finally the song comes on again.

The 12 o'clock train, Oh, oh, oh, you...

My mother frowns.

Our thoughts and greetings go out to the family of the martyr.

'This is the workers' station,' Abdelfettah explains to us.

'*Shalom, shal ...*'

'Do you know Hebrew, Abdelfettah?' I ask.

'Of course.'

'Be-yom khameshi. *Forces targeted Islamic Jihad offices in Jabalia.*'

Suddenly, the electricity turns off and we are cast into a sea of darkness. Little Nasreen calls out, 'Hey! Will someone light a candle? I want to see Auntie!'

My mother calls out: 'Sit down and be quiet—you've already talked enough for two people tonight. The Jews cut the power because they want to keep me from seeing your uncle Walid. They think we have too much time left, and they want us to say our goodbyes now. May God shut off the water in their throats. Please, God—just this once, for me?'

Abdelfettah adds, 'What did I tell you, Abu Fadi? Israel is conspiring against you and your mother. It's personal.' Somewhere in the darkness, we hear a flat colourless laugh. Amal slips through the gloom into the kitchen and returns with a pair of long candles. She places one on the ground in front of me, and another on the other side of the room.

Brother Namiq, Deir El-Balah is under fierce attack by Apache helicopters ...

'Where's Abu Hatem right now?' I wonder aloud. I pick up my mobile and call him. *The number you are trying to reach is not available right ...*

'No one is answering, Mama!'

'Call your cousin Suad,' my mother suggests. 'She went with them. They were going to drop her off on the way.'

245

'Hello, Umm Ayman? We're worried about Abu Hatem. Do you know where they are?'

'I'm worried too, cousin. They're at Mahfouza Checkpoint. He says the checkpoint is closed—and there are so many cars stuck there, the road is blocked in both directions. They're under attack right now.'

The electricity comes back on as suddenly as it went off. Under the glaring light, each of us rubs our eyes, hoping to get the shadows out.

By 1 in the morning, my mother and I are alone. Emad and Abdelfettah said goodbye and hugged me. Amal and I exchanged a few words of parting from across the room, then she picked up Nasr and followed her husband out of the door. I hugged their daughter Nasreen and gave her a kiss. As she ran to catch up with her parents, she asked: 'When are you coming back, Uncle?'

'Next year, I hope,' my mother says for me. '*Inshallah*, he's going to bring his whole family next time. Isn't that so, son?'

There was nothing to say but '*inshallah*'.

Shafiq, the last bachelor, had already left before them. He said he had to wake up early for work, then got up and said goodbye.

Here were are, by ourselves, my mother and I. I decide to ask her about something that has been bothering me for years. 'Mama, there's something I've wanted to ask for a long time. And I want you to tell me the truth.'

'Anything, son. I have nothing to hide from you.'

'Remember the acacia that used to stand over father's grave.'

'Of course I do. Nothing was kinder to him in death than that tree.'

'Mama, there were embroidered silk handkerchiefs hanging in the branches. Women's handkerchiefs. Who was it who put them there, Mama?'

'Ah. The handkerchiefs. You noticed them? I'll tell you the whole story. One day your father came home from work. As soon as I saw him, he took out an embroidered handkerchief from his pocket. He handed it to me and said: "That Jaffan woman gave this to me, Umm Walid. I didn't want to hide it from you. She's married, you know. When she gave it to me, I didn't want to give it back to her. I didn't want to embarrass her, but I told her not to do it again. The woman went away and never came back. The handkerchief sat in my pocket for two weeks before I admitted that it should go to you."'

'Were you jealous, Mama?'

'Of course, I was jealous. But I always trusted your father. When he passed away, God have mercy on him, I used to hang handkerchiefs on the branches for him. But I always held on to the one he gave me.'

'Do you know who the woman was?'

'God keep her safe and hidden. Everything turned out for the best.'

I decide not to tell her what my grandfather told me so many years ago about Sawsan al-Ghandour. I do not want to rekindle the embers of doubt she has managed to bury so deep. The trust she placed in my father is an impenetrable mountain.

Just before 10 am, Abdelfettah and I get into his little car and head toward the Beit Hanoun crossing. We pass through the empty streets of Jabalia and Beit Lahia. It is as if last night's death shadow still hovers over the place. Like everyone else in the two towns, we both expect an early morning ground assault to come along and take care of the unfinished business of hours ago. We expect to see tanks creeping into town at any moment.

When we reach Beit Hanoun, there are no tanks or troops to be found. The crossing is completely empty except for a pair of Palestinian security officers smoking and chatting with one another behind their desks.

Abdelfettah and I embrace one last time, then I walk over to the officers. I hand one of them my passport and he writes some notes. Then he picks up a walkie-talkie, and says something in Hebrew to the other side. From what I can gather, he is telling them that there is a British passport holder who wants to come through. A few minutes go by, then the man indicates that I can pass. Unescorted, I walk down the long corridor toward Israel.

Epilogue

I get into London around 10 pm. I am exhausted from all the travel and from all the security procedures I underwent at Ben Gurion, which were all the worse for my having come from Gaza. The whole time I was there, I was treated like someone who was smuggling suicide bombers in his suitcase. I was welcomed into the departures line by a woman in her twenties. She interrogated me for at least ten minutes, her questions focused on what I had been doing in Gaza and who I had met there. The thing that most infuriated me was that she kept asking why my passport indicated that I had been born in Ashdod. At first I ignored the studied stupidity of her questions, but eventually decided to give her something she could worry about for the rest of her life. I told her I was born before the state of Israel was even founded. I told her that, judging by our ages, I was more grown up than her country. The woman got angry and fled when a co-worker called her over. I was handed over to another security officer. This woman began to ask me the same set of questions, as if they both had studied the same lessons on the harassment of travellers at the same school. After a while, she stopped asking questions, and I stopped giving answers. I loaded my suitcase onto the X-ray machine, but a third girl stepped in to block me—confirming that her scorn for Palestinians was as discriminating as the rest of her colleagues'.

I went from the baggage inspection to another kind of inspection, this one performed by a handsome, well-dressed young man who asked me, with excessive politeness, to step away from my bags. He said he would go through them item by item and that he would personally put everything back in its place when he was through. He wiped down everything in my bag, and put the device on my passport as well—perhaps to search for anthrax spores in the pages inside.

All that took two hours. And then there was an additional hour of waiting in front of another window for my exit visa.

I was able to sit by myself on the airplane. I did not have to sit there feeling like I was under surveillance by the person sitting next to me. The five hours went by without any Dana Ahova. No drama, no sobbing. I spent most of the time finishing *Cruel Weddings*. Little Ludo grows up inside a sanatorium. In my mind, I compare it to the mental institution I just left. I am grateful that my sanity is still intact.

When I arrive home, Julie is there waiting for me with open arms. She hugs me tightly, and in her arms the three weeks of separation dissolve. I tell her about my mother and about everyone else, conveying their greetings, hugs and kisses. I promise to fill her in later about everything that happened during my trip, including how the experience messed with my novel. I tell her about the surprise meeting with Adel El-Bashity.

Later, I check my emails and see that on the morning I left Gaza, I had received a second email from Dana. In it, she tells me she is returning to London in two days to attend a 'Jewish documentary film festival', and that if I am free, she would enjoy meeting up with me.

Then she continues: if we are to meet again, she must tell me something very important. And she writes:

Meeting you on the plane was the first time I'd ever spoken to a Palestinian up close. I could not say what I wanted to say then, so I write to you now. Maybe you noticed my reaction when you told me you were on your way to Gaza.

I wanted to tell you what I know of Gaza. First let me tell you a little more about Dani, who left me and Israel as you know, but also left me a great experience at the time. Dani was drafted into the IDF. The idea of facing off against rock-throwing kids every day made him crazy. He wrote to me: 'Why do we go on prolonging this occupation, and until when? Has anyone ever been able to occupy another country for ever?' I admit that his words touched something deep in me.

When I heard about the incident at the Erez crossing, I wondered where you were and sent you that last email. Your fleeting ghost carried me back to the time of my military service. Like Dani, in a way. You see, I, too, was in the army. I, too, went to Gaza. I will never forget it, my night at the Amal Refugee camp: it is burnt into my memory.

On the evening I am speaking about, just before nightfall, I left the base to catch a breath of fresh air. The afternoon was perfect. I watched the sun disappear behind sand dunes, dragging along behind it the last rays of orange light. My friend Pinchas suddenly appeared from a long way off, gripping in one hand the strap of his leather shoulder bag, and in the other he carried his gun. I went back to the base to tell Eila, another soldier and Pinchas' girlfriend, that he had returned from Natanya. She was cleaning a rifle. She put it down and rushed out to meet him.

About 10am the next day, demonstrations broke out in the Amal camp near the base. They came right up to where we were. And suddenly rocks began to rain down on us. Pinchas was hit in the head with a stone. We told him to get to the clinic, which was right there, but instead he opened up with his gun, firing live rounds right into the crowd. A girl fell to the ground not far from where we were. The crowd split as everyone began to run back to the camp.

Without thinking, I ran to the girl. I bent over her and took her pulse. Immediately I realized that I was too late.

She was twelve.

A few days later, we were surprised to learn that Pinchas had been transferred to the Golan Heights. Eila began to lose it. When the girl was killed, she had had no problem keeping it together, but now she went berserk. As Eila started looking for ways

*to join her boyfriend in the Golan, I started looking
for a way out of that madness. I lost both Pinchas
and Eila on that ugly morning, and I began to think
I would lose myself too if I stayed. The spectre of
the girl began to follow me everywhere. And inside
me, a voice began to cry out, the voice of the girl
asking me: Why didn't you stop him? Weren't you
standing right next to him? Why didn't you take his
gun away?*

*I made the decision to get out of the Gaza Strip
then and there. I demanded a transfer anywhere.
I was ready to do anything, anything to get out of
Gaza.*

That's it. Now I've told you.

Dana

Walid looks at the monitor for a long time before replying. Dana's story does not shock him. In fact, he
thinks, it seems to logically follow – or precede – the
long story she had recounted on the flight to Tel Aviv,
about her relationship with the Ukrainian she named
'Dani'. It also follows the cold logic of the country
Dana calls home ...

He sends her a reply, but only to suggest a meeting
the day after her arrival, in the evening at an Italian
restaurant in Southbank Centre. On his way to work
next morning he receives an email from Dana in return,
warmly welcoming his invitation and saying she's
looking forward to meeting him again. Neither of them

has mentioned this new long story she has just told him; neither of them has to.

The following day, Walid finishes work just before 6 pm. Leaving his office, he walks past Green Park Station toward Piccadilly Circus. He enjoys watching the evening descend gently across the city, and feels as though he is seeing the beauty of twilight for the first time. He catches glimpses of faces in the street crowds. He arrives at Piccadilly Circus and descends the stairs into the Underground. He hears footsteps behind him, and voices that seem to call him, and he falters and turns around: there are only two girls there, dragging heavy suitcases on rollers and speaking loudly.

He sprints down the remaining stairs toward the platform, and leaps into the carriage. The doors close and the train begins to speed out of the station. Within seconds, the dark tunnel has swallowed Walid.